"Matilda, will you marry me?"

The handsome Dutchman's blue eyes gleamed as he continued, "Consider the alternatives and think about it. I believe that we may have a pleasant life together, even if unromantic. You will never be bored."

Matilda sat and looked at Rauwerd, her thoughts running in all directions like frightened mice running from a cat. He had harped on the unromantic aspect and she regretted that, for she was a romantic girl, and to marry a man who regarded her as a good friend and nothing more was lowering — to say the least.

But Rauwerd was honest about it, and though she wasn't in love with him, she did like him....

Betty Neels is well-known for her romances set in the Netherlands, which is hardly surprising. She married a Dutchman and spent the first twelve years of their marriage living in Holland and working as a nurse. Today she and her husband make their home in a small ancient stone cottage in England's West Country, but they return to Holland often. She loves to explore tiny villages and tour privately owned homes there, in order to lend an air of authenticity to the background of her books.

Books by Betty Neels

HARLEQUIN ROMANCE

Don't miss any of our special offers. Write to us at the following address for information on our newest releases.

Harlequin Reader Service
901 Fuhrmann Blvd., P.O. Box 1397, Buffalo, NY 14240
Canadian address: P.O. Box 603,
Fort Erie, Ont. L2A 5X3

The Doubtful Marriage

Betty Neels

Harlequin Books

TORONTO • NEW YORK • LONDON
AMSTERDAM • PARIS • SYDNEY • HAMBURG
STOCKHOLM • ATHENS • TOKYO • MILAN

Original hardcover edition published in 1987
by Mills & Boon Limited

ISBN 0-373-02891-1

Harlequin Romance first edition February 1988

CHAPTER ONE

THE waiting-room was full and smelled of wet raincoats and old Mr Stokes's eucalyptus cough lozenges; he had chronic bronchitis and treated himself with a variety of cures from the chemist until he finally gave in and went to the doctor. He sat glowering at the people around him, his eyes on the green light over the surgery door; he was next in.

But when the light changed it flickered on and off, a signal for the girl sitting behind the desk in the corner to go into the surgery. She got up without haste to obey the summons, aware that Uncle Thomas wanted her to see to Mrs Spinks's varicose ulcer. She smiled at him as she went in; smiled, too, at his patient and urged that lady to the curtained-off cubicle behind his desk. Mrs Spinks eased her stout person on to the chair and extended her leg on to the stool provided for her.

'Busy this morning,' she commented. 'We keep you on the go, don't we, love?'

The girl was bending over her leg, dealing with it with kind, gentle hands. She was a very pretty young woman, with chestnut hair piled on top of her head, large brown eyes, a straight nose and a generous mouth. She was wearing a white overall with a blue belt buckled in silver and when she stood up it was apparent that she was tall and splendidly shaped.

She said in a pleasant voice, 'Oh, I think the doctor

and I wouldn't know what to do with ourselves. When are you to come back, Mrs Spinks?'

She helped her to her feet and ushered her out through the door behind them, tidied the cubicle and went back into the surgery where her uncle was dealing with Mr Stokes. There was nothing for her there; Mr Stokes was barely half-way through his testy list of grievances while her uncle listened patiently, as he always did.

In the waiting-room a dozen pair of eyes watched her as she crossed to the desk again. The doctor's niece had been living in the village since she was a little girl; they all knew her well. A nice young lady she had grown into, they considered, and one of them as it were, despite her years at the London hospital where she had gone for her training. High time she was married; she and the squire's only son had been courting for the last year or two, and even though he was away from home a good deal that was time enough for them to get to know each other. At least, that was what the ladies of the village said. They held old-fashioned views about such matters—a year or so to get acquainted, another year's engagement and then a proper wedding in church with the banns called and bridesmaids. Anything less wasn't seemly.

Matilda smiled impartially upon them all, sifted through the patients' cards and counted heads. If Mr Stokes didn't finish his grumbling pretty smartly, morning surgery was going to be very behindhand, and that meant that her uncle's morning round would be even later, which would lead inevitably to gobbled sandwiches and a cup of coffee before afternoon surgery. That did him no good at all; he worked too hard and long hours, and just lately she had begun to worry about him. He wasn't a young man and was all she had in the world; he had been father and mother to her since the day she had gone to live with him after her parents had been killed in a car accident.

Mr Stokes came out, still muttering, and she ushered the next patient in.

Finally the waiting-room was empty and she poked her head round the surgery door. 'Coffee in the sitting-room, Uncle. I'll clear up while you're on your round.'

He was sitting at his desk not doing anything, a tired, elderly man, short and stout and almost bald, with a cheerful, chubby face and bright blue eyes.

'A busy morning, Tilly.' He got up slowly. 'Another couple of months and it will be spring and we'll have nothing to do.'

'That'll be the day! But it will ease off soon—January and February are always busy, aren't they?' She urged him gently to the door. 'Let's have that coffee before it gets cold. Would you like me to drive? I can clear up in ten minutes.'

'Certainly not—almost all the visits are in the village anyway. You've got the list? There may be a call from Mrs Jenkins—the baby is due.'

They sat down on either side of the log fire and Tilly poured the coffee. The room was comfortable, albeit shabby, but the silver on the old-fashioned sideboard shone and the furniture was well polished. As she put down the coffee-pot, an elderly grey-haired woman came in.

'I'm off to the butchers,' she observed. 'A couple of lamb chops, Miss Matilda, and a nice steak and kidney pudding for tomorrow?'

'Sounds splendid, Emma. I'll give you a hand as soon as I've tidied the surgery.' As Emma trotted off, she added, 'I don't know how we'd manage without Emma, Uncle. I can't imagine life without her.' Which wasn't surprising, for Emma had been housekeeping for her uncle when she had gone to live with him.

She filled his coffee cup again and sat back, her feet tucked under her, planning what she would do in the garden once the weather had warmed up a little.

'How would it be . . .' she began, to be interrupted by her uncle.

'I forgot to tell you, I've had a letter from someone who was at St Judd's when I was there—oh, it must be ten years ago. He was my houseman for a time—a splendid fellow and very clever. We've kept up a casual friendship since then but we haven't met—he's a Dutchman and has a practice in Holland, I believe, though he comes over to England fairly frequently. He's in London now and wanted to know if he might call and see me. I phoned him last night and asked him for the weekend.'

It was her uncle's free weekend and Matilda had cherished one or two ideas as to what they would do with it. Now they were to be burdened by some elderly foreigner who would expect a continental breakfast and want coffee instead of tea. Matilda, who in all her twenty-six years had never set foot outside Great Britain, tended to think of Europeans as all being cast in the same mould.

She said hastily, 'That'll be nice for you, Uncle. I'll get a room ready. When do you expect him?'

'Tomorrow, after lunch. Friday's clinic shouldn't be too full—there's not much booked so far, is there?—and I'll be free after that. You can entertain him if I get tied up.' He added a shade anxiously, 'He's a nice chap.'

'I'll make some scones,' said Matilda. The steak and kidney pudding would never do, on the other hand she could slip down to the butchers and get more steak . . . Calabrese and carrots, mused Matilda silently, and creamed potatoes; there was enough rhubarb forced under the old bucket at the end of the garden to make a pie. They could have beef on Saturday instead of Sunday; perhaps he would go on Sunday morning. 'Does he know this part of the country, Uncle?'

'I don't believe so. It'll make a nice change from London.'

She was left on her own presently to get one of the bedrooms in the roomy old house ready for the guest and go to the kitchen and tell Emma.

'Dutch?' questioned Emma, and sniffed. 'A foreign gentleman; probably have faddy ways with him.'

'Well, he oughtn't to be too bad,' mused Tilly, 'if he comes over to London fairly often, and Uncle said he does. I'll go and pull some leeks, shall I?' She pulled on an old jacket hanging behind the kitchen door. 'I'll get a few apples in at the same time—we might have an apple crumble . . .'

When she got back she saw to the waiting-room and the surgery, made sure that the room was ready for her uncle's guest and went down to the kitchen to help with lunch.

It was after morning surgery on the following day that the phone rang. It was Mr Jenkins, sounding agitated.

'It's the missus, started the baby and getting a bit worked up.'

It was Mrs Jenkins's fourth; Uncle Thomas wouldn't be back for half an hour at least and the Jenkins's farm was outside the village. Moreover, it seemed to Tilly that Mr Jenkins sounded as worked up as his wife.

'The doctor's out,' she said soothingly. 'I'll jump on my bike and come and have a look, shall I? I'll leave a message for Uncle; he shouldn't be long.' She heard Mr Jenkins's heavy sigh of relief as she hung up.

She warned Emma to let her uncle know as soon as he came in, fetched her midwifery bag, put on the elderly coat once more and cycled through the village to the farm.

A far cry from the clinically clean delivery rooms of the hospital, she thought, going into the cluttered warm kitchen. Mr Jenkins was hovering over a boiling kettle on the stove, under the impression that, since this was the common practice on the films in similar circumstances, it was the correct thing to do.

'Hello,' said Tilly cheerfully. 'Upstairs in bed, is she?'

He nodded. 'Carrying on, too. Good thing the kids have gone over to Granny's.'

'I'll go up, shall I?' Tilly went up the wooden staircase at the end of the passage and knocked on the half-open door at the top. Mrs Jenkins was sitting on the bed, looking apprehensive.

She looked more cheerful when she saw Tilly, who put her bag down and sat down beside her, put a comforting arm round her and asked pertinent questions in a calm voice.

Presently she said, 'Well, I don't suppose it'll be long—shall I have a look? And how about getting into bed?'

The bouncing baby boy bawling his head off with satisfying vigour arrived with commendable speed. The doctor, arriving some ten minutes later, pronounced him to be in splendid health, declared his satisfaction as to Mrs Jenkins's well-being, observed that he might leave Tilly to make her patient comfortable, and left again to see the last of his patients.

It was almost one o'clock by the time Tilly had seen to Mrs Jenkins, bathed the baby, shared a pot of tea with the proud parents and got back on her bike. Mrs Jenkins's sister would be arriving very shortly and she would be in good hands.

'See you this evening,' called Tilly, and shot off down the lane.

She was a bit dishevelled by the time she reached home; there was a fierce wind blowing, and a fine, cold rain falling, and she had had to cycle into it. She propped the bike against the wall outside the kitchen door and hurried into the house, kicking off her shoes as she went and unbuttoning her coat. There was no one in the kitchen; she went through to the hall and opened her uncle's study door, still struggling with the coat. Her uncle was standing by his desk, and sitting in the big leather chair by the fire was a man. He got to his feet as she went in, an extremely tall man, broad-shouldered and heavily built. Somewhere in the thirties, she guessed fleetingly, and handsome, with lint fair hair and heavy-lidded blue eyes. Surely not their visitor?

But he was.

'Ah, Matilda, there you are.' Her uncle beamed at her, oblivious of her untidy person. 'Here is our guest, as you see, Rauwerd van Kempler.'

She said, 'How do you do,' in her quiet voice and had her hand engulfed in his large firm grasp. He greeted her pleasantly and she thought peevishly that he might have come at a more convenient time.

The peevishness sparked into temper at his bland, 'I'm afraid I have arrived at an awkward time.' His glance took in her shoeless feet and her damp face and her hair all over the place.

'Not at all,' said Tilly coolly. 'I got tied up with the Jenkins's baby.' She looked at her uncle. 'I hope you haven't been waiting for me to have lunch?'

'Well, dear, we had a good deal to talk about, you know, over a drink.' Her uncle studied her carefully. 'I expect you'd like to tidy yourself—I'll pour you a glass of sherry while you're doing it.'

Tilly, aware that the Dutchman was studying her as carefully as Uncle Thomas, took herself out of the room.

Very deliberately she did her hair and her face and changed into a skirt and sweater. On the way to the study she went to the kitchen to see if Emma needed any help. She didn't, so Tilly joined the two men, accepted the sherry and made polite conversation about the weather. Her uncle looked at her once or twice, puzzled by her aloofness; she was puzzled by it herself.

Dr van Kempler had an easy way which made conversation simple, and he had good manners; it was obvious that he and her uncle had a lot in common and plenty to talk about, but he was careful to keep the talk general and when Uncle Thomas began to reminisce, headed him off with unobtrusive ease.

The two of them went off to the study when they had had their coffee, leaving her to clear the table and help Emma with the washing up. She agreed that their visitor seemed a nice enough man. Nice wasn't the right word, she mused silently; a milk-and-water word which had no bearing upon his good looks and vast proportions. She would like to get to know him better, a wish instantly suppressed as disloyal to Leslie, who would be home for the weekend and expect her up at the Manor, ready for one of their lengthy walks in which he delighted whenever he was home. He was a rising young barrister, working hard in London, and they didn't see much of each other. They had known each other for years now and she couldn't remember when the idea of marrying him first entered her head. She supposed it was his mother who had planted it there—a rather intimidating matron who saw in Tilly a girl who could be moulded into the kind of wife she wanted to have for her son. Not quite the same background, she pointed out to her husband, but Dr Groves had a good solid country practice and a delightful house, set in grounds of an acre or two, most conveniently running alongside one of the boundaries of the Manor grounds. Nothing could be more suitable. She was proud of Leslie's work as a barrister; at the same time she was terrified that he would meet some quite unsuitable girl in London and marry her out of hand. Tilly, known to her since childhood, was eminently preferable.

Tilly had more or less accepted the situation. She liked Leslie, was fond of him without loving him; if she regretted giving up her hospital career in order to help her uncle she had never said so. She owed him a lot and he hadn't been well for some time; she was able to take some of his work on to her own shoulders and, although she didn't think about it very often, she supposed that she would continue to do so until he retired and she married Leslie. She was a fortunate girl, she knew that, but at the same time there was the disturbing thought, buried deep, that something was missing from her life: romance; and being a normal pretty girl, she wanted that. It was something she wouldn't get from Leslie; he would be a good husband and once they had settled down she would forget the romantic world she dreamed of. She was old enough to know better, she chided herself briskly, and, indeed, she wasn't quite sure what she wished for.

She went down to the village presently; supper would need to be augmented by a few extras. It was still raining and very windy as she went round the side of the house to the front drive. The doctor's car was standing there: a Rolls-Royce in a discreet dark blue, and she stopped to admire it. Undoubtedly a successful man, their guest.

The doctor, watching her admire his car from the study window, admired her.

Mrs Binns, in the village shop, already knew as much about Dr Groves's guest as Tilly. The village was very small but there were scattered farms all around it and, although many of the villagers went into nearby Haddenham to shop, Mrs Binns was still the acknowledged source of local gossip.

'So 'e's 'ere, Miss Matilda, and an 'andsome gent from what I hear.' She sliced bacon briskly. 'Nice bit of company for the doctor. Speaks English, does 'e?'

'Very well, Mrs Binns. I'd better have some cheese . . .'

'Mr Leslie coming this weekend?'

'Yes. I hope it will stop raining.'

People were more interesting than the weather from Mrs Binns's point of view. 'He'll be glad to get 'ome, I'll be bound. Named the day yet, 'ave you, Miss Matilda?'

'Well, no.' Matilda sought for something harmless to say which Mrs Binns wouldn't be able to construe into something quite different. 'We're both so busy,' she said finally.

Which was true enough, but, when all was said and done, no reason for not getting engaged.

She started back up the lane and met Dr van Kempler. He said cheerfully, 'Hello, I've come to carry your basket. Is there a longer way back or do you mind the rain?'

'Not a bit. We can go down Penny Lane and round Rush Bottom. It'll be muddy . . .' She glanced down at her companion's highly polished shoes.

'They'll clean,' he assured her laconically. 'What do you do in your spare time, Matilda?'

'Walk, garden, play tennis in the summer. Go to Thame or Oxford to shop.'

'Never to London to go to a play or have an evening out?' He glanced at her from under heavy lids. 'Your uncle mentioned your ... fiancé, is he?'

'Not yet. He is a barrister and he'd rather spend his weekends here than in London.' She got over the stile to Rush Bottom. It was her turn to ask questions. 'Are you married, Dr van Kempler?'

'No, though I hope to be within the next months. Life is easier for a doctor if he has a wife.'

She was tempted to ask him if that was his reason for marrying, but she didn't know him well enough and, although she thought he was friendly, she sensed that he could be quite the reverse if he were annoyed. He didn't want to talk about himself; he began to talk about her work as practice nurse with her uncle. That lasted until they got back to the house.

She was in his company only briefly after that; there was the evening visit to Mrs Jenkins before she phoned the district nurse in Haddenham who would take over for the weekend. When she got back, Emma, normally so unflappable, was fussing over the supper. 'Such a nice young man,' she enthused. 'I must do me best.'

'You always do, Emma,' Tilly assured her, and then, 'He's not all that young, you know.' She paused over the egg custard she was beating gently over the pan of hot water. 'All of thirty-five—older than that ...'

'In 'is prime,' declared Emma.

Her uncle had no surgery in the morning. After

breakfast he and his guest disappeared into his study, leaving Tilly free to clear the table, make the beds and tidy the house, having done which she got into her newest tweed skirt and quilted jacket, tied a scarf over her dark locks and walked through the village to the Manor.

Leslie always drove himself down late on Friday evening, too late to see her; besides, as he had pointed out so reasonably, he needed a good night's sleep after his busy week in town. He would be waiting for her and they would decide where they would walk, and afterwards he would go with her to her uncle's house, spend five minutes talking to him and then go home to his lunch. It was a routine which never varied and she had accepted it, just as she had accepted Sunday's habitual visit to morning church and then drinks at the Manor afterwards. Sometimes she wished for a day driving with Leslie, just the two of them, but he had pointed out that his mother had come to depend on his weekly visits, so she had said nothing more.

He was in the sitting-room, glancing through the papers, when she reached the Manor and for some reason his, 'Hello, old girl,' annoyed her very much. Normally she was an even-tempered girl and sensible; better a sincere greeting shorn of glamour than a romantic one meaning nothing.

She paid a dutiful visit to his mother and they had their walk, he talking about his week and she listening. He was still explaining a particularly interesting case when they reached her uncle's house, to find him and the Dutch doctor sitting in the drawing-room, deep in discussion. They got to their feet as Tilly and Leslie

went in and the doctor introduced Leslie to his guest
and offered him a drink. It irked Tilly considerably that
Leslie should refuse and, worse, give her a careless pat
on the shoulder and a ''Bye, old girl,' as he took his
leave. With a heightened colour she gave the Dutchman a defiant look and met a bland face which gave
nothing away; all the same she was sure that he was
amused.

She wouldn't be seeing Leslie until the next
morning; he was taking his mother over to Henley to
see old friends and would stay there to dine, something
which she had to explain to her uncle at lunch.

'Pity you couldn't go, too. Better still, have a day out
together ...'

Tilly, serving the custard, said calmly, 'I dare say we
shall when the weather's better.'

'Well, if you've nothing else to do, you can go with
Rauwerd to Oxford. He has a mind to renew his
acquaintance with the colleges.'

Dr van Kempler came to her rescue very nicely. 'I'd
be delighted if you would,' he said. 'I didn't mention it
because I supposed that you would be spending the day
with—er—Leslie, but I should enjoy it much more if I
had a companion.'

'Oh, well, then I'll come.' Tilly smiled at him. 'Were
you there?'

'Yes, years ago. There was a splendid tea-room in the
High Street ...'

'It's still there.'

'Then perhaps we might have tea there?'

The afternoon was a success. The rain didn't bother
the doctor. They walked down High Street to
Magdalen Bridge and looked at the river, stopped to

stare at Tom Tower, peered around Magdalen College,
studied Radcliffe Camera, the Sheldonian Theatre and
the Rotunda and then had their tea in a tea-room which
the doctor swore hadn't altered so much as by a
teaspoon since he was there. They walked back
presently to where he had parked the car and drove
home. He was nicer than she had at first thought,
mused Tilly, sitting back in the comfort of the Rolls,
and it had been pleasant to spend an afternoon well
away from the village. A pity that she and Leslie
couldn't take time to do that sometimes ... She
dismissed the thought as disloyal.

The doctor wasn't going until after tea on Sunday;
Tilly got up early, made a trifle for lunch so that Emma
would be free to see to the main course, whisked
together a sponge cake as light as air, helped to get
breakfast and went to church, Uncle Thomas on one
side, Dr van Kempler on the other. Their pew was on
the opposite side of the aisle to the Manor pew; she
caught Leslie's eye and gave him a warm smile, and
when the service was over joined him in the porch.

Mrs Waring, waiting with him, had to be introduced
and said at once in her slightly overbearing manner,
'You must come up for a drink. You, too, Thomas—
you are so seldom free.'

There was a path through the churchyard which led
to the Manor grounds, and Mrs Waring led the way
with the two doctors, leaving Tilly and Leslie to follow.

For some reason which Tilly couldn't quite understand she didn't enjoy herself; everything was exactly
as it always was on a Sunday morning, with Mrs
Waring dominating the conversation while they sat

around in the rather grand drawing-room sipping the rather dry sherry Tilly had never really enjoyed. Dr van Kempler had behaved with the ease and unselfconscious poise of someone to whom good manners are as natural as breathing, yet behind that bland face she was sure that he was laughing, not at them, she conceded, but at some private joke of his own.

The talk followed a well-worn routine: Mrs Waring's opinion on world affairs, a severe criticism of the week's work done or mismanaged by the government and a detailed résumé of the village life since the previous Sunday. When she paused for breath her husband muttered, 'Quite so, my dear,' and everyone murmured, for there was no chance to speak. It surprised Tilly when, having come to the end of her diatribe, Mrs Waring began to question Dr van Kempler. Was he married? Where did he live? Exactly what work did he do?

She had met her match. The Dutchman answered her politely and told her nothing at all. Tilly, who had her ears stretched to hear his replies, was disappointed. Mrs Waring tapped him playfully on an exquisitely tailored sleeve. 'You naughty man,' she declared, 'you're not telling us anything.'

'I have nothing to tell,' he assured her with grave courtesy, 'and I much prefer to hear of your English village life.'

'Well, yes, I flatter myself that I take an active part in it. What do you think of our two young people? I cannot wait for Matilda to become my daughter.'

'You will indeed be most fortunate.' His voice was as bland as his face.

Tilly blushed and looked at her shoes. It was a relief when Uncle Thomas declared that they must be off home otherwise Emma would have their lunch spoilt.

After lunch she saw little of the doctor. He spent the afternoon with her uncle and after tea got into his splendid car and drove away. His goodbyes had been brief but warm to her uncle and equally brief but considerably cooler towards herself.

She watched the car disappear down the lane with mixed feelings: regret that she couldn't get to know him better, and relief that she never would. He wasn't only the handsomest man that she had ever set eyes on; she was sure he was someone she instinctively trusted, even though she was still not sure if she liked him.

The house seemed empty once he had gone. She listened to her uncle contentedly reflecting on his weekend, but when she asked where the doctor lived and what exactly he did, he was vague.

'You should have asked him,' he pointed out. 'I dare say we'll be seeing more of him; he's often in England these days and we still have a great deal to say to each other. He has become successful—modest about it, too.' He chuckled. 'Didn't give much away to Mrs Waring, did he?'

For that matter, mused Tilly, getting ready for bed later that evening, he hadn't given much away to her, either. He was as much a stranger as when she had encountered him. Yet not a stranger; it puzzled her that she felt as though she had known him for a lifetime.

'What nonsense,' said Tilly loudly and jumped into bed.

There was precious little time to think about him during the next few days. Mrs Jenkins and the infant Jenkins, both flourishing, still needed visiting, there were several bed-ridden patients who required attention once if not twice daily, and morning and evening surgeries were overflowing by reason of the particularly nasty virus 'flu which had reached the village. The days went fast and by the end of the week she and her uncle were tired out.

The weekend was a succession of anxious phone calls from people who had stubbornly gone on working through the week and then decided to call in the doctor on Friday evening, and morning surgery on Saturday was no better. There was no question of Sunday church; Tilly drove her uncle from one patient to the next through rain and sleet and hail and high winds. They had a brief respite until the early evening, when Tilly went to visit a couple of elderly patients in the village and her uncle was called out to a farm some miles away.

She was back before him, helping Emma with supper, ready with a hot drink for him when he got in.

He sat down in his chair by the fire and she thought how ill he looked.

'Coffee with a spot of whisky in it. You look all in, Uncle.'

She sped away. When she got back she took one look at him motionless in his chair. She put the tray down on the table and felt for a pulse which was no longer there. He had always told her that he hoped to die in harness, and he had.

* * *

Everyone who could walk, and quite a few who couldn't but had cajoled friends and family to push wheelchairs, came to the funeral. Tilly, stunned by the suddenness of it all, found that their concern for her uncle's death almost shattered the calm she had forced upon herself. Everyone had been so kind and Leslie had come from London to attend the funeral. Mrs Waring had begged her to go and stay at the Manor house but this she refused to do; for one thing she couldn't leave Emma on her own and for another, Mrs Waring, though full of good intentions, was overpowering.

'Of course, you and Leslie can marry now,' she pointed out with brisk kindness. 'You can live in your uncle's house and Leslie can commute each day; nothing could be more convenient.' A remark which, well-meaning though it was, set Tilly's teeth on edge.

She was aware of disappointment that there had been no letter or message from Dr van Kempler. There had been a notice in *The Times* and the *Telegraph* as well as a short item in the *Lancet*. Once or twice she caught herself wishing that she had him there; she needed someone to talk to and somehow, when Leslie came, it was impossible to talk to him. She wanted to talk about Uncle Thomas and she sensed that he was avoiding that.

He had spoken of their marriage, echoing his mother's suggestions, and Tilly, who above all wanted to be loved and cherished and allowed to cry on his shoulder, felt lost. To his rather colourless suggestion that they should marry quietly within the next month or so she returned a vague answer. It was too soon to think of marrying; she had to get used to being without

Uncle Thomas and she didn't mind living alone in his house for the time being. She had said that defiantly to Leslie and his mother, sitting on each side of her giving her sound advice. When she said it she had no idea that she wasn't going to have the chance to do that anyway.

Uncle Thomas's sister came to the funeral and with her came her son and his wife. Tilly had only a fleeting acquaintance with her aunt and almost none with her cousin and his wife. They uttered all the very conventional phrases, behaved exactly as they should and were a little too effusive towards the Warings, and, when the last of the doctor's friends and patients had gone, followed Tilly and the family solicitor into the doctor's study.

Half an hour later they led the way out again. Her aunt had the smug look of someone who had found a ten pound note in an empty purse and her cousin Herbert had an air of self-righteous satisfaction which he made no effort to conceal now the funeral was over. He moved pompously across the hall and into the sitting-room where he sat down in his uncle's chair.

Tilly eyed him with sternly held-back feelings. He wasn't in the least like her dear Uncle Thomas: of only average height, with a waistline already going to seed despite his thirty or so years; portly was the word which crossed her mind, and overbearingly conceited. He smoothed his thinning dark hair back from his forehead and gave her a superior smile.

'Well, well, that's been a surprise to you, I dare say, Matilda.' He glanced at his wife, Jane, a rather timid colourless young woman. 'We shall have to make room for our cousin, won't we, my dear? I would be the last person to disregard the wishes of Uncle Thomas.'

He looked around him complacently. 'This is a comfortably sized house. There is no reason why you shouldn't stay here, Matilda, even keep your room until you marry Leslie Waring.' He added, 'I could do with a cup of tea—such a very busy day ...'

Tilly said tonelessly, 'I'll get it,' and went out of the room to the kitchen where she found Emma crying over a plate of cakes. 'Oh, Miss Tilly, whatever came over your uncle? The dear man couldn't have thought ...'

Tilly put the kettle on. 'Well, yes, he did, and I'm sure he thought he was doing the right thing. He hasn't seen Herbert for years; he wasn't to know what he's like.' She shuddered. 'I'm to stay here until I marry and when I do, Emma, you're coming with me.'

'Of course I will, Miss Tilly. Me stay 'ere with that nasty man? You and Mr Waring find a nice 'ouse and I'll look after it for you.'

She wiped her nice elderly face and put the cakes on the tea tray. 'I dare say it won't take too long.'

'Well, no. I'd told Mrs Waring that I didn't want to get married for a month or two, but now things are altered ...'

Her aunt and Herbert and Jane were driving back to Cheltenham that evening. He had work to do, Herbert had told her pompously, but he would write and tell her their plans within the next few days. He owned a small factory on the outskirts of the town which he supposed he could run just as well from the house he had inherited as his own smaller, modern one in Cheltenham. 'If that isn't satisfactory I can sell this place—it should fetch a good price.'

Tilly didn't say anything—what would be the good? Uncle Thomas had so obviously meant it to stay in the family and for Herbert to provide a home for her for as long as she would need one. She bade them a polite goodbye and went thankfully to help clear away the tea things and then phone Leslie.

To her disappointment he had already gone back to London. 'He won't be back until the weekend, my dear,' his mother told her. 'Why not give him a ring? I expect you want to tell him about the will—so very satisfactory that you can settle on a date for the wedding now.'

Tilly held her tongue; everyone would know sooner or later but she wanted Leslie to be the first. She would phone him in the morning; better still, she would drive up to town and see him.

She dressed carefully in the morning, taking pains with her face and hair and wearing a suit Leslie had said that he liked. It was still early when she left and she was at his rooms soon after ten o'clock. His clerk was reluctant to accept her wish to see Mr Waring without delay.

'It's most important,' said Tilly and smiled at him with charm, so that he picked up the receiver to announce her.

Leslie looked different—she supposed it was his sober suit and manner to go with it—but he greeted her warmly enough. 'Sit down, Tilly—I've fifteen minutes or so before I go to court. Have you decided to marry me after all? I thought you would once you heard your uncle's will.'

There was no sense in beating about the bush. She said quickly, not mincing matters, 'He left the house to my cousin Herbert, with the wish that I make it my home until I marry.'

The sudden frown on Leslie's face frightened her a little. 'You mean to say that your uncle has left you nothing?'

'Five hundred pounds. He made the request that Herbert would pay me a fitting allowance ...'

'Can the will be overset? I'll see your solicitor. Why, you're penniless.'

Tilly stared at him. 'That makes a difference to our plans?' she asked, and knew without a doubt that it did.

CHAPTER TWO

LESLIE looked at his wristwatch. 'I must go. This is something which we must discuss quietly. I'll come home as usual tomorrow and we can talk everything over with my mother and father.'

'I haven't told them as I didn't think there was any need to. After all, they have been urging us to get married now that Uncle is dead.' Tilly's voice was calm but inside she shook and trembled with uncertainty. She had expected Leslie to reassure her, tell her that she had no need to worry, that he would take care of her future. Now she wasn't sure of that.

Leslie looked uncomfortable. 'Look, old girl, we'll sort things out tomorrow.' He got up and came round his desk and kissed her cheek. 'Not to worry.'

But of course she worried, all the way back home and for the rest of the day. The house seemed so empty, the surgery and the waiting-room empty, too, waiting until Monday when the medical centre in Haddenham were to send over one of their members to take morning surgery until such time as a new doctor came to the village or things were reorganised and a small surgery was set up and run by the Haddenham doctors. In any case, thought Tilly, she would never be needed any more. Not that that would matter if she married Leslie. For the first time she put her nebulous thoughts into words. 'Leslie might not want to marry me now.'

She had a phone call from Mrs Waring the next

morning; would she go over for dinner that evening? Leslie hoped to be home rather earlier than usual, and they had a lot to discuss. There was a letter from Herbert, too; he and Jane and her aunt would be coming down and would go over the house and make any changes needed at the beginning of the week. Jane and his mother would move in very shortly, he wrote, and he would commute until such time as the sale of his own house was dealt with. The letter ended with the observation that she was probably looking for a nursing post.

She put the letter tidily back into its envelope. It wasn't something she could ignore; it was only too clear that that was what she was expected to do. Unless Leslie married her out of hand . . .

Something it was only too obvious he didn't intend to do.

His, 'Hello, old girl,' was as friendly as it always had been and his parents greeted her just as they had always done for years, yet there was an air of uneasiness hanging over the dinner-table and a deliberate avoidance of personal topics. It was only when they were drinking their coffee in the drawing-room that the uneasiness became distinctly evident.

'I hear,' said Mrs Waring, at her most majestic, 'that your uncle's will was unexpected. Leslie tells me that there is no way of contesting it.'

Tilly glanced at Leslie. So he had spoken about it with his parents, had he? He didn't look at her, which was just as well, for her gaze was fierce.

'It has always been our dearest wish,' went on Mrs Waring in a false voice, 'that you and dear Leslie should marry—your uncle's property matched with ours, the house was ideal for a young couple to set up home; besides, we have known you for so many years. You would have been most suitable.' She sighed so deeply that her corsets creaked. 'It grieves us very much that this cannot be. You must see for yourself, my dear, that our plans are no longer practical. We are not wealthy; Leslie needs to marry someone with money of her own, someone who can—er—share the expenses of married life while he makes a career for himself. Luckily there is no official engagement.'

Tilly put down her coffee cup, carefully, because her hands were shaking. 'You have put it very clearly, Mrs Waring. Now I should like to hear what Leslie has to say. After all, it's his life you are talking about, isn't it?' She paused. 'And mine.'

She looked at Leslie, who gave her a weak smile and looked away. 'Well, old girl, you can see for yourself . . . Where would we live? I can't afford a decent place in town. Besides, I'd need money—you can't get to the top of the ladder without it . . . meeting the right people and entertaining . . .' He met Tilly's eye and stopped.

'I can see very well,' said Tilly in an icy little voice, 'and I am so thankful that the engagement isn't official. If it were I would break it here and now. A pity I have no ring, for I would fling it in your face, Leslie.'

She got to her feet and whisked herself out of the room, snatched her coat from the hall and ran out of the house.

She couldn't get home fast enough; she half ran, tears streaming down her cheeks, rage bubbling and boiling inside her. It was fortunate that it was a dark evening and there was no one around in the village to see her racing along like a virago.

Emma took one look at her face, fetched the sherry from the dining-room cupboard, stood over her while she drank it, and then listened patiently.

'Well, love, I'd say you're well rid of him. If a man can't stand up against 'is ma, he'll make a poor husband. As to what you're going ter do, get a job, Miss Tilly. I'm all right 'ere—yer uncle saw ter that, bless 'is dear 'eart. But don't you go staying 'ere with that cousin of yours—no good will come of it, mark my words.'

Tilly went to church on the Sunday morning, her chin well up, sang the hymns loudly and defiantly, wished the occupants of the Manor pew a chilling good morning and went home to compose a letter to the principal nursing officer of her training school. She hadn't worked in a hospital for some years now, but she had been in the running for a sister's post when she left; she could hardly expect that, but there might possibly be a staff nurse's job going.

Two days later Herbert, Jane and her aunt arrived without warning. Herbert sat back in her uncle's chair, looking smug. 'It seemed a good idea if Mother and Jane should get used to the idea of living here. I'll come at weekends, of course. The house in Cheltenham is up for sale with most of the furniture—I'll get the stuff we shall want to have here sent down when I have time to arrange it. I'm a busy man.'

Tilly said tartly, 'Too busy to let us know that you were coming? And even if you were, surely Jane could have telephoned?'

'I deal with all the domestic arrangements.' He smoothed his hair back and half closed his eyes. 'Jane isn't strong.'

Jane, thought Tilly, was as strong as the next girl, only her strength was being syphoned off her by her great bully of a husband.

Herbert waved a hand, presumably in dismissal. Tilly stayed right where she was sitting. 'So who does the housekeeping?' she asked sweetly.

'Oh, Mother, I suppose, though you might carry on for a day or two until she's found her way around.'

'I might and then I might not,' said Tilly. 'You have been at great pains to remind me that this is no longer my home—I'm here on sufferance, aren't I? You haven't considered me at all; why should I consider you? I'm sure Aunt Nora will manage beautifully.'

She took herself off to the kitchen, shutting the door on Herbert's outraged face. There was a lot of coming and going—Aunt Nora and Jane finding their way around, thought Tilly waspishly. She went to find Emma crying into the potatoes which she was peeling.

Over a cup of tea they faced the future. Tilly would have liked a good cry but she couldn't; Emma had to be comforted and given some kind of hope.

'Has the postman been? There may be a letter from the hospital—I wrote for a job. As soon as I'm settled Emma, I'll find a flat and we'll set up house. Just hang on here, Emma dear, and I promise everything will be all right. There's the postman now.'

There was a letter. Tilly read it quickly and then a second time. There was no job for her; regretfully, there was the full quota of nurses and no way of adding to it, but had Tilly thought of applying for a job at one of the geriatric hospitals? They were frequently understaffed; there was no doubt that she would find a post at one of them.

It was a disappointment, but it was good advice, too.
Tilly got the *Nursing Times* from her room and sat
down there and then and applied to three of the most
likely hospitals wanting nursing staff. Then, while
Emma was seeing to lunch, she went down to the post
office and posted them. She met Mrs Waring on the
way back and wished her a polite good day and that lady
made as if to stop and talk.

'I'm in a great hurry,' said Tilly brightly. 'My cousin
and his wife have arrived unexpectedly.'

'Moving in already?' asked Mrs Waring in a shocked
voice. 'Tilly, what are you going to do? Leslie's so
upset.'

Tilly went a little pale. 'Is he? Goodbye, Mrs
Waring.'

She smiled in Mrs Waring's general direction and
raced off home. If Leslie was upset, he knew what to
do . . .

Only he didn't do it. He neither telephoned her nor
wrote, which made life with Jane and her aunt just that
much harder to bear. So that when there was a letter
from a north London hospital asking her if she would
attend an interview with a view to a staff nurse's post in
a female geriatric ward, she replied promptly and two
days later presented herself at the grim portals of a huge
Victorian edifice, very ornate on the outside and
distressingly bare within.

She followed the porter along a corridor painted in
margarine-yellow and spinach-green, waited while he
tapped at its end on a door and then went in. She hadn't
much liked the look of the place so far; now she felt the
same way about the woman sitting behind the desk, a

thin, acidulated face topping a bony body encased in stern navy blue.

'Miss Groves?' The voice was as thin as its owner.

'Yes,' said Tilly, determinedly cheerful. 'How do you do?'

'I am the Principal Nursing Officer.' The lady had beady eyes and no make-up. 'I see from your letter that you are seeking work as a staff nurse. A pity that you have not worked in a hospital for a while. However, your references are quite in order and we are willing to give you a trial. The ward to which you will be assigned has forty patients. I hope you don't mind hard work.'

'No. Would I be the only staff nurse?'

The beady eyes snapped at her. 'There are part-time staff, Miss Groves. We take a quota of student nurses for a short period of geriatric nursing—they come from various general hospitals—and we also have nursing auxiliaries.' She paused, but Tilly didn't speak, so she went on, 'You will do day duty, with the usual four hours off duty and two days free in the week. It may be necessary from time to time to rearrange your days off. you will be paid the salary laid down by the NHS, monthly in arrears, and your contract may be terminated at the end of the month by either of us. After that you will sign a contract for one year.'

'I should like to see the ward,' suggested Tilly, and smiled.

She got no smile in return, only a look of faint surprise.

'Yes, well, that can be arranged.'

In answer to a phone call, a dumpy little woman in a checked uniform joined them. 'Sister Down,' said the Principal Nursing Officer, 'my deputy.' She turned the pages of some report or other on the desk and picked up her pen. 'Be good enough to let me know at your earliest convenience if you are accepting the post, Miss Groves.' She nodded a severe dismissal.

The hospital was left over from Victorian days and as far as Tilly could see no one had done much about it since then. She followed the dumpy sister along a number of depressing corridors, up a wide flight of stone stairs and into a long narrow ward. It was no good, decided Tilly, gazing at the long rows of beds down each side of it, each with its locker on one side and on the other side its occupant sitting in a chair. Like a recurring nightmare, she thought as they traversed the highly polished floor between the beds to the open door at the end. It led to the ward sister's office, and that lady was sitting at her desk, filling in charts.

She greeted Tilly unsmilingly. 'The new staff nurse? I could do with some help. How soon can you come?'

She looked worn to the bone, thought Tilly, not surprising when one considered the forty old ladies sitting like statues. There were two nursing auxiliaries making a bed at the far end of the ward and a ward orderly pushing a trolley of empty mugs towards another door. Tilly didn't know what made her change her mind; perhaps an urge to change the dreary scene around her. Music, she mused, and the old ladies grouped together so that they could talk to each other, and a TV . . .

'As soon as you want me,' she said briskly.

She didn't tell her aunt or Jane, but confided in Emma, who had mixed feelings about it.

'Supposing you don't like it?' she wanted to know. 'It sounds a nasty ol' place ter me.'

'Well, it's not ideal,' agreed Tilly, 'but it's a start, Emma, and I can't stay here.' Her lovely eyes took fire. 'Aunt has changed all the furniture round in the drawing-room and she says an open fire is wasteful there, so there is a horrid little electric fire in there instead. And she says Herbert wants all the books out of Uncle's study because he is going to use it as an office. So you see, Emma, the quicker I settle in to a job the better. I've a little money,' she didn't say how little, 'and I'll go flat hunting as soon as possible. It's not the best part of London but there'll be something.'

She spoke hopefully, because Emma looked glum. 'You do realise that it will be in a street and probably no garden? You'll miss the village, Emma.'

'I'll miss you more, Miss Tilly.'

Leslie came to see her on the following evening, and without thinking she invited him into the drawing-room. She had nothing to say to him, but good manners prevailed. She was brought up short by her aunt, sitting there with Jane.

She wished Leslie a stiff good evening and raised her eyebrows at Tilly.

'Will you take Mr Waring somewhere else, Matilda? Jane and I were discussing a family matter.' She smiled in a wintry fashion. 'I'm sure it is hard for you to get used to the idea that you can't have the run of the house any more, so we'll say no more about it.'

Tilly clamped her teeth tight on the explosive retort she longed to utter, ushered Leslie out into the hall and said in a voice shaking with rage. 'Come into the kitchen, Leslie. I can't think why you've come, but since you're here we can at least sit down there.'

'That woman,' began Leslie. 'She's ... She was

rude, to me as well as you.'

Not quite the happiest of remarks to make, but Tilly let it pass.

She sat down at the kitchen table and Emma gathered up a tray and went to set the table in the dining-room. No one spoke. Tilly had nothing to say and presumably Leslie didn't know how to begin.

'You can't stay here,' he said at length. 'You're going to be treated like an interloper — it's your home.'

'Not any more.'

'Well, your uncle meant it to be; surely your cousin knows that?'

'Herbert is under no legal obligation,' Tilly observed.

Leslie stirred uncomfortably. 'I feel . . .' he began, and tried again. 'If circumstances had been different . . . Tilly, I do regret that I am unable to marry you.'

She got up. 'Well, don't.' She kept her voice cheerful. 'I wouldn't marry you if you were the last man on earth, Leslie. Besides, I've got a job in London; I shall be leaving in a few days.'

She watched the relief on his face. 'Oh, that is good news. May I tell Mother? She will be so relieved.'

He went awkwardly to the door. 'No hard feelings, Tilly?'

She opened the door and stood looking at him. 'If you ask a silly question you'll get a silly answer,' she told him.

When he had gone she sat down again and had a good cry; she was a sensible girl, but just at that moment life had got on top of her.

Herbert arrived the next day, stalking pompously through the house, ordering this to be done and that to be done and very annoyed when neither Tilly nor Emma took any notice of his commands.

'I expect co-operation,' he told her loftily when he asked her to move a chair from one room to another.

'If you wish any of the heavy furniture to be moved, then I suggest you do it yourself, Herbert. After all, you are a man, aren't you?' Tilly said it in a placid voice which stopped him doing more than gobble like a turkey cock. It was an opportunity to tell him that she would be leaving; she had had a letter from the hospital asking her to report for duty in two days' time—a Monday. It didn't give her much time to pack up but, if she didn't manage it all, Emma could finish it for her and send the rest on.

When it came to actually leaving, it was a wrench. The nice old house had been her home for almost all of her life and she had been very happy there. Besides, there was Emma. She promised to write each week and to set about finding somewhere to live just as soon as possible.

The nurses' home at the hospital was as gloomy as its surroundings. Tilly was shown to a room on the top floor with a view of chimney pots and one or two plane trees struggling to stay alive. At least they would provide some green later on to relieve the predominant red brick. The room was of a good size, furnished with a spartan bed, a built-in dressing-table and a wardrobe with a small handbasin in one corner. There was no colour scheme but the quilt on the bed was a much washed pale blue. There was a uniform laid out on it, blue and white checks, short-sleeved and skimpily cut. With it was a paper cap for her to make up. She stood looking at it, remembering the delicately goffered muslin trifle she had worn when she had qualified, and the neat blue cotton dress and starched apron.

She was to go to the office as soon as she had unpacked and changed into her uniform. The Principal Nursing Officer was there to bid her a severe good afternoon and speed her on her way to the ward. 'Sister Evans is waiting for you, Staff Nurse.'

It was barely three o'clock but the monumental task of getting forty old ladies back into their beds had already begun. As far as she could see, Tilly could count only four nurses on the ward, and one of those was Sister, who, when she saw her, left the elderly lady she was dealing with and came to meet her.

She nodded in greeting and wasted no time. 'I'm off duty at five o'clock, Staff Nurse. I'll take you through the Kardex and show you where the medicines are kept. You do a round after supper at seven o'clock. Supper is at six o'clock; ten patients have to be fed. You'll have Mrs Dougall on with you—she's very reliable and knows where everything is kept. There's a BP round directly after tea. The trolley's due now, but you'll get a few calls before the night staff come on at eight.' Sister Evans smiled suddenly and Tilly saw that she was tired and doing her best to be friendly.

'You'll be able to manage? I'm having days off—I've not had any for two weeks. The student nurses aren't due to come for another two weeks and one of the part-time nurses has left. There'll be one in tomorrow after dinner, so that you can have the afternoon off.' She was sitting at the desk, pulling the Kardex towards her. 'I'm very sorry you're being thrown in at the deep end.'

Tilly stifled a desire to turn and run. 'That's all right, Sister, I'll manage. This Mrs Dougall, is she trained?'

'No, but she's been here for five years, longer

than any of us, and she's good with the old ladies.'
She nodded towards a chair. 'We'll go through the
Kardex ...'

The rest of the day and the two which followed it
were like a nightmare. Mrs Dougall was a tower of
strength, making beds, changing them, heaving old
ladies in and out of their chairs, a mine of information.
When she wasn't on duty Tilly had to manage with the
three other nursing auxiliaries, whose easy-going ways
tried Tilly's temper very much. They were kind
enough, but they had been there long enough to regard
the patients as puppets to be got up, fed and put back to
bed. Which wasn't the case at all. At least half of them
could have been at home if there had been someone to
look after them; the patient despair in their eyes almost
broke Tilly's soft heart. It was always the same tale—
daughter or son or niece didn't want them, because
that would mean that they would have to stay at home
to look after them. Tilly was of the opinion that a good
number of the old ladies were perfectly capable of
looking after themselves with a little assistance, but the
enforced idleness and the hours of sitting in a chair
staring at the patients opposite had dulled their energy
and blunted their hopes. However strongly she felt
about it, there wasn't very much that she could do. She
suspected that a new principal nursing officer might
alter things; it was lack of staff and the adhering to the
treatment used several decades earlier which were the
stumbling blocks. The geriatric wards in her own
training school had been light and airy, decorated in
pastel shades, and the patients had been encouraged to
take an interest in life.

*   *   *

Sister Evans looked ten years younger when she came back on duty.

'You coped?' she asked, and added, 'I see that you did. We'll be able to have days off each week now, thank heaven.'

At Tilly's look of enquiry she said, 'No staff, you see. They won't stay because Miss Watts won't allow us to change the treatment. She ought to retire—she's not well—but she won't. I'd have left months ago but my fiancé is in Canada and I'm going out to him as soon as he is settled.' She looked at Tilly. 'You're not engaged or anything like that?'

'No, Sister.'

'Well you ought to be, you're pretty enough. If you get the chance,' went on Sister Evans, 'don't let a sense of duty stop you from leaving. As soon as Miss Watts retires all the things you need doing will be done.' She opened the Kardex. 'Now we'd better go through this . . .'

The week crawled its slow way to Sunday and on Monday Tilly had her days off. She wanted very much to go to her uncle's house but that wouldn't be possible; she wouldn't be welcome. She had written to Emma in the week and mentioned that she would have two days off a week and explained why she wouldn't be returning to her old home. To her delight Emma had written back; why didn't Miss Tilly go to Emma's sister who lived at Southend-on-Sea and did bed and breakfast? The fresh air would do her good.

Tilly had never been to Southend-on-Sea and certainly not in early March, but it would be somewhere to go and she longed to get away from the hospital and its sombre surroundings. She phoned Mrs Spencer, and found her way to Liverpool Street Station early on Monday morning. It was an hour's journey and the scenery didn't look very promising, but the air was cold and fresh as she left the station and asked the way to Southchurch Avenue. Mrs Spencer lived in one of the streets off it, not ten minutes from the Marine Parade.

The house was narrow and on three floors, in a row of similar houses, each with a bay window framing a table set for a meal and a sign offering 'Bed and Breakfast'. In the summer it would be teeming with life, but now there was no one to be seen, only a milk float and a boy on a bicycle.

Tilly knocked on the front door and it was flung open by a slightly younger version of Emma.

'Come in, my dear,' invited Mrs Spencer, 'and glad I am to see you. Emma wrote and I'm sure I'll make you comfy whenever you like to come. Come and see yer room, love.'

It was at the top of the house, clean and neat, and, provided she stood on tiptoe, it gave her a view of the estuary.

'Now, bed and breakfast, Emma said, but it's no trouble to do yer an evening meal. There's not much open at this time of the year and the 'otels is expensive. There's a sitting-room and the telly downstairs and yer can come and go as yer please.'

The kind creature bustled round the room, twitching the bedspread to perfection, closing a window. 'Me 'usband works at the 'ospital—'e's a porter there.' She retreated to the door. 'I dare say you could do with a cuppa. I got a map downstairs so that you can see where to go for the shops, or there's a good walk along the cliffs to Westcliff if you want a breath of fresh air.'

Half an hour later Tilly set out, warmed by her welcome and the tea and armed with detailed instructions as to the best way to get around the town. It was a grey morning but dry; she walked briskly into the wind with the estuary on one side of her and the well-laid-out gardens with the houses beyond on the other. By the time she reached Westcliff she was glowing and hungry. There were no cafés open along the cliff road so she turned away from the sea and found her way to Hamlet Court Road where she found a coffee bar and she had coffee and sandwiches. Then, since Mrs Spencer had warned her that it was nothing but main roads and shops when away from the cliffs, she walked back the way she had come, found a small café in the High Street and had a leisurely tea, bought herself a paperback and went back to Mrs Spencer's.

Supper was at half-past six when Mr Spencer got back home; sausages and mash and winter greens and apple pie with cups of tea to follow. It was a pleasant meal with plenty to talk about, what with Mr Spencer retailing his day's work and Mrs Spencer's careful probing into Tilly's circumstances. 'Emma didn't tell me nothing,' she assured Tilly, 'only of course we knew that you worked for your uncle . . .' She smiled at Tilly so kindly that she found herself telling her all about it, even Leslie. But she made light of it and, when she could, edged the talk back to Emma.

It was a fine clear morning when she woke and after breakfast she helped with the washing-up, made her bed and went out. This time she walked to Shoeburyness, in the other direction, found a small

café for her coffee and sandwiches and started to walk
back again. She hadn't realised that it was so far—all of
five miles—and half-way back she caught a bus which
took her to the High Street. Since she had time on her
hands she looked at the shops before going back to Mrs
Spencer's. It was poached egg on haddock for supper,
treacle tart and more tea. She ate everything with a
good appetite and went to bed early. She was on duty at
one o'clock the next day and she would have to catch a
train about ten o'clock.

It had been a lovely break, she reflected on the train
as it bore her to London, and Mrs Spencer had been so
kind. She was to go whenever she wanted to, 'though in
the summer it's a bit crowded—you might not like it
overmuch, love. Kids about and all them teenagers
with their radios, but it'll stay quiet like this until
Easter, so you come when you want to.'

She would, but not for the next week; she would
spend her two days going to the local house agents and
looking over flats.

Going back on duty was awful but the awfulness was
mitigated by Sister Evans's real pleasure at seeing her
again. They had been busy, she said, but she had felt a
bit under the weather and would have her days off on
Saturday and Sunday and have a good rest.

Tilly, once Sister had gone off duty for the
afternoon, went round the beds, stopping to chat while
she tidied up, fetched and carried, and coaxed various
old ladies to drink their tea. Some of them wanted to
talk and to hear what she had been doing with her free
days and she lingered to tell them; contact with the
outside world for some of them was seldom and most of
them knew Southend-on-Sea.

The later part of the afternoon was taken up with the Senior Registrar's visit. He was pleasant towards the patients but a little bored, too, and not to be wondered at since he had been looking after several of them for months, if not years.

'There are one or two temps,' Tilly pointed out, 'And a number of headaches.'

"Flu? Let me know if they persist. Settling down, are you?'

'Yes, thank you.'

He nodded. 'This isn't quite your scene, is it?'

She had no answer to that so it was just as well that he went away.

By the end of the week a number of old ladies were feeling poorly.

'I said it was 'flu.' The registrar was writing up antibiotics. 'You'll need more staff if it gets much worse.'

Two extra nurses were sent, resentful of having to work on a geriatric ward instead of the more interesting surgical wing, but it meant that Sister Evans could have her weekend off. She had been looking progressively paler and more exhausted and Tilly went on duty earlier on the Friday evening so that she could go off duty promptly.

'I'll do the same for you, Staff,' said Sister gratefully. 'You've got days off on Tuesday and Wednesday.'

However, Sister Evans wasn't on duty when Tilly got on to the ward on Monday morning. Instead there was a message to say that she was ill and Staff Nurse Groves would have to manage. The Principal Nursing Officer's cold voice over the phone reminded her that she had two extra nurses.

'We are all working under a great strain,' added that lady. 'You must adapt yourself, Staff Nurse.'

Which meant, in fact, being on duty for most of the day, for various of the old ladies added their symptoms to those already being nursed in their beds, so that the work was doubled, the medicine round became a major chore and the report, usually a quickly written mixture of 'no change', or 'good day', now needed to be written at length.

By the end of the week Tilly was looking very much the worse for wear; hurried meals, brief spells of off duty, and the effort of keeping a cheerful comforting face on things were taking their toll. The last straw was the Principal Nursing Officer informing her that Sister Evans was to have a further week's sick leave and that Tilly could not have her days off until she was back.

Tilly tackled the Registrar when he came on to the Ward later that day. 'Forty old ladies, more than half of them ill—there's me, Staff Nurse Willis who comes in three times a week from two o'clock until six, and there is Mrs Dougall, two auxiliaries and the two extra I've been lent. With off duty and days off I'm lucky to have more than two on at a time. You must do something about it.'

He didn't want to know. He was a good doctor, but overworked, and there were acutely ill patients on the medical side. He said unwillingly, 'I'll see what I can do.'

He wasn't very successful. Not only was she refused any extra help, but she was sent to the office where she was told that at the end of the month her services would no longer be required. 'You are not suitable for the post,' said the Principal Nursing Officer, 'although I am sure that you have done your best.'

Matilda, since she had been given the sack already, felt that she could speak her mind. 'What you mean is that my ideas of nursing geriatric patients don't fit in with yours. They are human, you know, they still think and talk and take an interest in the things going on about them, but you haven't moved with the times, you treat them as though they were workhouse patients, sitting in rows until they die of boredom.' She was so carried away that she actually shook an admonitory finger at the incensed lady sitting behind the desk. 'Many more staff, a little painting and decorating, organised occupational therapy, a chance for the more active patients to walk around . . .'

'You will leave at the end of the month, Staff Nurse.'

'Yes, I will. I shall also write to the local MP, the Regional Nursing Board, and anyone else I can think of. The geriatric unit is an absolute disgrace and you should be ashamed of yourself!'

She got herself out of the office, shaking with rage and presently with fright. Probably she would be struck off, or whatever they did to staff nurses who dared to argue with their superiors.

Off duty was quite out of the question. It wasn't Staff Nurse Willis's day to come in and though Mrs Dougall was perfectly capable of running the ward she wasn't allowed to. Tilly plunged into a round of chores with brief respites for meals and at the end of a long day, sat down to write the report. The one nurse she had on duty had gone to her supper, so Tilly took her Kardex into the ward and sat at the table where she could see everyone. The old ladies were quiet now, dozing away the first early hours of the evening, and she wrote busily, making her tired brain remember the day's happenings. She was almost finished when the door at the far end of the ward opened and Dr van Kempler came in.

CHAPTER THREE

MATILDA, her mouth slightly open, watched him make his unhurried way towards her. When he reached the table he stood quietly looking at her, his look so intent that she put a hand up to her hair and said stupidly, 'I'm a bit untidy; I've had a very busy day ...'

'I only heard this morning.' He had ignored her remark; she might never have made it. 'I came at once. I'm so sorry—he was a good man. Why are you here, looking ...' he paused, 'so tired? And why are you working in this place? Why have you left your home?'

'Questions, questions,' said Tilly peevishly. 'I've no time to answer them. There's the report to finish and the night staff will be here in ten minutes.'

'In that case, once you have dealt with it, we will go somewhere quiet and you shall answer them.'

He drew up a chair and sat down and when Tilly said, 'You can't do that,' he said calmly,

'A friend of mine is on the committee here. I arranged to come and see you; some gorgon on the telephone did her best to prevent me.'

'The Principal Nursing Officer. She has given me the sack.'

'Yes? That's good.'

There was a flutter of movement as the night nurses came on to the ward; two auxiliaries, and one of those would only stay until the patients had been settled for the night.

'I'll stay here while you give the report,' said Dr van Kempler. He spoke with a quiet authority which took it for granted that she would do just that; so she did, with all her usual calm, her quiet voice omitting nothing, while at the back of her head there was a rising tide of disbelief. She had imagined it all; doctors who weren't attached to hospitals didn't just walk on to wards and sit down coolly as though they had a right to do so. She got to the end of the report and stole a look out of the open office door. He was still there, sitting relaxed like a man at his own fireside.

She went with the nurse to take a final look at the ill patients and found him walking beside her as she left the ward. At the head of the staircase he said, 'I'll be at the front entrance—is fifteen minutes long enough for you?'

She pushed back a dark curl. 'I'm tired . . .'

'We will go somewhere quiet.' The smile he gave her was very kind.

It would be a waste of time arguing with him. She nodded and turned away to go to the nurses' home.

She looked a fright. She cast one look in the mirror on the dressing-table and tore out of her uniform. She had showered, got into a tweed suit, done the best she had time for with her face and hair, and pushed her tired feet into high heels. It had been a grey day and it was dark now; she hoped she would be warm enough as she hurried down to the front entrance.

Dr van Kempler was lounging against a Grecian pillar bearing the bust of some long-dead gentleman

with side whiskers and a stern mouth. He reached the
door as she did and opened it with a cheerful, 'You were
quick—the car is here.'

Her tired head seethed with questions but it was too
much bother to utter them. She sat in blissful comfort
while he drove away from the hospital and the rows of
small, dull streets until they reached Oxford Street. He
turned off at St Giles's Circus and presently stopped at
Neal Street Restaurant, smallish and quiet, somewhere, she thought gratefully, where her suit wouldn't
look too out of place.

They had a table in a corner and the doctor spoke for
the first time. 'What would you like to drink while we
choose, Matilda?'

She sipped her sherry and studied the menu, aware
that she was hungry.

'Did you have lunch?' he asked casually.

'Well, a sandwich . . .'

'Iced melon?' he suggested. 'And how about *sole
véronique* to follow?'

The food was delicious and beyond a modicum of
conversation the doctor spoke little, leaving her to
enjoy the fish and the splendid dish of vegetables which
went with it—new potatoes, broccoli and artichoke
hearts. A hot soufflé covered in chocolate sauce
followed and it wasn't until she had finished these and
the coffee had been put on the table that he sat back and
said quietly, 'Now, from the beginning, Matilda.'

The hock had loosened her tongue. Besides, it was
marvellous to be able to talk to someone; someone who
would listen, she felt instinctively, and who had known
Uncle Thomas well.

It was fairly difficult to begin, but once she had started, words came easily. She laid the whole sorry story before him in a matter-of-fact voice and when she had finished she asked him, 'More coffee? I'm afraid it's not very hot now.'

He ordered another pot with a gently raised hand. 'Thank you for telling me. I have to go back to Holland,' he didn't tell her that he was flying back, leaving his car in London, 'but something shall be done, I promise you.'

'You are coming back?' She had no idea that she sounded so anxious, and his bland face and heavy-lidded eyes told her nothing.

'Oh, yes.' She took comfort from his smile.

'How did you know where I was?' she asked.

'I telephoned your uncle. Someone—your aunt?— told me what had happened. They were not very forthcoming, so I drove down and saw Emma.' He caught her questioning look. 'Very early in the morning, before anyone was about. She told me where you were.'

'You went to a lot of trouble.' She studied his quiet face.

'Your uncle was my friend. I'm going to take you back now.' His eyes searched her face. 'You're all right?'

She nodded. 'I'm very grateful—just to talk . . .'

He nodded and smiled, the kind smile which changed his rather austere face.

He saw her into the hospital, lifted his hand in casual farewell and drove away, leaving her deflated. She remembered as she undressed that she hadn't asked him why he was bothering about her. Perhaps he felt an obligation towards Uncle Thomas. In which case, she thought sleepily, I must make it clear that he need not be. I'm quite able to look after myself.

She was far too busy with the old ladies to give herself any thought at all. The sad state of affairs they were in couldn't last for ever, she comforted herself, as, gamely seconded by Mrs Dougall, she plunged into yet another day's work. She was tired and she had a dull headache and everything took twice as long as it should have done; from the other side of the bed they were making Mrs Dougall said flatly, 'You've got the 'flu Staff Nurse.'

'I'm a bit tired, that's all. I think we're over the worst of it; another week and we'll be back to normal, hopefully. If only we had more nurses ...'

Her headache got worse as the day wore on. She had gone off duty for a couple of hours in the afternoon while the part-time staff took over, and she had slept heavily, waking unrefreshed. Filling in the Kardex, waiting for the night staff, she decided not to go to supper; Panadol and bed made more sense.

She felt worse in the morning but there was nothing for it but to go on duty; there would be only three of them—herself, Mrs Dougall and another nursing auxiliary. She had just finished taking the report from the night nurse when Mrs Dougall answered the phone.

'You're wanted in the office, Staff,' she said, and added *sotto voce*, 'and don't let her flatten you.' She cast an anxious eye over Tilly's white face. 'You don't look fit to be here—it's a crying shame.'

Tilly went carefully out of the ward and down the stairs, holding her head very carefully still because it ached so atrociously. At the office door she took a deep breath, knocked and went in.

The Principal Nursing Officer wasn't there; there was a stout balding man sitting at her desk and beside him a thin man with a clever face. Standing a little apart was Dr van Kempler.

He stepped forward, took the door handle from her and shut the door, and offered her a chair, but he didn't speak. It was the man behind the desk who addressed her.

'Staff Nurse Groves, we owe you both an apology and an explanation.' He paused and looked carefully at her. 'You are very pale—that is no wonder. I must tell you on behalf of the whole hospital committee that we are very distressed to have been made aware of the situation here. It will be put right immediately. We have already arranged for agency nurses to supplement the staff; the Principal Nursing Officer has—er—gone on extended sick leave. I may say that we are happy to have secured the services of a most capable lady in her place. Things will be put right as soon as possible. I am told that you were dismissed—quite unfairly. We shall be only too happy to retain your services; you can rest assured that you will have no further fault to find with the administration.'

He had a sonorous voice; it went through Tilly's throbbing head like a sledgehammer. She caught a word here and there and when she looked at him he was all fuzzy round the edges. She frowned in her efforts to understand what he was saying. And what was Dr van

Kempler doing, standing there? She turned her head to look at him and winced with pain. Perhaps if she shut her eyes for a minute . . .

Dimly she heard Dr van Kempler speak. "Flu, and I'm not surprised. I'll take her home. I think you can take it from me that she won't be coming back.' He nodded at the thin man. 'Thanks for all the help, Dick.'

'Only too glad to have helped. And our thanks for bringing this state of affairs to light, Rauwerd. Keep in touch . . .'

Dr van Kempler nodded again, scooped Matilda up as though she had been a bundle of straw, and carried her, apparently without effort, through the hall and out of the entrance. The surprised porter who had opened the door followed him outside and opened the car door as well. The doctor arranged Matilda tidily in the front seat. 'Will you see someone about packing up Miss Groves's things and sending them to my house?' He scribbled in his notebook. 'Here is the address. Thanks.' A coin or two changed hands. 'As soon as possible.'

Matilda collected her wool-gathering wits. 'Nurses' home,' she muttered urgently, and then, remembering her manners, 'So sorry . . .'

The doctor didn't answer that but got into the car and drove off, away from the hospital, leaving the dull streets behind and finally stopping in a narrow elegant street close to Grosvenor Square. His house was the end one of a terrace, a small Regency cottage with spotless paintwork and shining windows. Its handsome front door opened as he drew up and Emma came down the steps.

'Have you got Miss Matilda there, sir?' she asked anxiously. 'Is she all right?'

He got out without haste. 'She's here, Emma. She has 'flu—she must go straight to bed. Is the room ready?'

'Oh, yes.' Emma trotted round the car and peered in at Matilda, who gazed back at her in a bemused way. Really, the strangest things were happening. It was a pity that she couldn't be bothered to think about them.

'Emma,' she said, 'why are you here and where am I?'

'Don't talk now,' advised the doctor, and since he sounded a little testy, she didn't. In any case, it was too much effort.

Thinking about it afterwards, she was vague as to what had happened. She was aware of Emma fussing round her, of being carried upstairs and of another elderly face peering down at her and voices talking quietly. She wasn't sure who got her into bed, only that its cool comfort was bliss. Someone gave her a drink, offered pills and then more drink and told her to go to sleep.

When she woke, the dull day was dwindling into dusk and her headache was bearable. She turned her head just to make sure and saw the doctor; he was sitting near her bed. He had a folder of papers on his knees and was writing, but he looked up as she moved and got up and came over to the bed.

'Feeling a little better?' And, when she nodded, 'No, don't talk—time enough to do that later. Emma will freshen you up and give you a drink and you'll go to sleep again.' He poured some water from the carafe on the table beside the bed. 'Take these now.'

She felt hot and cross, and when he left the room tears of tiredness and temper trickled down her cheeks. Emma, bearing a tray on which was a jug of lemonade, properly made from her own recipe, wiped her cheeks for her, washed her face and hands, then combed her hair and coaxed her to drink.

'There, there, my lamb, you'll feel better in the morning. Just you close your eyes now.'

'That's all very well,' said Matilda peevishly, 'but why are you here, Emma, and where are we?'

'Why, the doctor fetched me, sensible man that he is, and this is his house. Now do go to sleep, Miss Tilly.'

'I don't want to,' said Tilly a little wildly, 'not until someone's explained.'

Her hand was taken in a firm cool grasp. 'You have a high temperature,' said Dr van Kempler, sounding exactly like a doctor should when dealing with a recalcitrant patient. 'You will go to sleep now; tomorrow you will feel more yourself and you may ask all the questions you wish.'

He didn't let go of her hand, but sat down on the bed. 'I shall stay here until you are asleep,' he observed calmly.

'Oh, well, in that case,' mumbled Matilda and closed her eyes.

Incredibly, it was morning when she woke again. She lifted her head cautiously from the pillow and found her headache a mere echo of what it had been. She sat up in bed and looked around her. Emma was asleep in a big armchair, wrapped in a dressing-gown and with a blanket tucked around her. There was a small table by her with a shaded reading lamp on it; by its light and the glimmer of light around the curtains, Matilda inspected the room. It was of a fair size and very elegantly furnished with Regency period pieces, the curtains were old-rose watered silk with swathed pelmets and the bedspread matched them. Eaten up with curiosity, Matilda got rather gingerly out of bed. A peep from the window might give her some clue as to where she was. She crept across the carpeted floor and twitched the curtains very gently aside. It was still very early but the sky was clear and there was the promise of sun before long. She looked down on to a small garden, having high walls and paved round a small ornamental pool; there were flower beds around it and neatly trimmed grass. She studied it all slowly and craned her neck to see directly below the window, to encounter the doctor's upturned face.

It gave her quite a shock. She got back into bed, feeling guilty, and wondered about him. He had been in a thick sweater and slacks and there had been a dog with him, a very large and woolly German Shepherd dog, who had looked at her with the same intentness as his master.

It was a good thing that Emma woke up then, enquired anxiously how she felt and bustled away to get tea, waving aside Matilda's pleas to be told where she was and why. 'You'll be told soon enough, now you're better, love,' said Emma, pulling back curtains and folding a blanket.

She closed her eyes the better to think and then opened them at the gentle tap on the door. The doctor came to the bed and picked up her arm and took her pulse and remarked pleasantly, 'You're better.'

'That's a very large dog,' said Matilda.

'Dickens. We had just returned from our morning walk.' The blue eyes studied her. 'You are, of course, dying of curiosity.'

'Yes, oh yes, I am. How did I get here and where am I anyway, and how did Emma get here and how did you know ...'

He smiled slowly. 'You are better, aren't you?' He got up from where he had been sitting on the edge of the bed and took Emma's tray from her as she came through the door. 'If we perhaps have our tea together while I answer your questions?'

He glanced at Emma, who smiled at him and said, 'I'll get dressed, doctor, if it's all the same to you.'

He poured their tea, put another pillow behind Matilda and offered her a cup. 'Emma has been a splendid source of information,' he told her, 'but I'm sure she could not know the whole, I hope that you will tell me exactly what has happened. But you have questions of your own.'

She was feeling herself better with every passing minute. 'Where am I?'

'At my house.' He added the address. 'I brought you here yesterday morning. Your things came yesterday afternoon; Emma has unpacked them.'

'But there was no need for that. It was very kind of you to look after me, but I'm quite able to go back to the nurses' home.'

'But you are not going back,' said Dr van Kempler baldly. 'You will remain here.'

She gaped at him. 'Stay here? Of course I shan't—I

must get back on duty.' She frowned suddenly. 'Oh, I was sacked, wasn't I? I'd forgotten.' She finished her tea. 'Those men in the office with you. I didn't feel very well; I'm not sure what they were talking about.'

'They were offering you an apology and an explanation, Matilda. It seems that no one had realised that the Principal Nursing Officer was on the verge of a nervous breakdown and quite unfit for her task.'

'How did you know?'

He shrugged. 'I made it my business to find out. I told you that I knew someone on the hospital committee.'

'Emma—how on earth did Emma get here?'

'I fetched her and she won't be going back.'

'You fetched her? But didn't Herbert object?'

The doctor's smile came and went. 'Er, yes, he did. But of course he had no say in the matter.'

Matilda looked at him sitting there. He really was vast; she quite saw that Herbert wouldn't have stood a chance. His blustering would have gone unheeded and the sheer size of the doctor would have reduced him to reluctant agreement.

'Emma's pleased,' she said.

'I understand so.' He poured more tea and she took the cup, frowning while he watched her.

'But where will she go? And you said I wasn't going back to the hospital. Where am I going?'

'Ah, yes. Well, supposing we discuss that presently. I think that now you must have your breakfast and sleep again for a while. You may get up after lunch if you feel like it, but I must warn you that you are going to feel off colour for a few days.' He put down his cup and saucer.

'I must change and go to the hospital.'

'Which one?'

He mentioned a famous teaching hospital and she said, puzzled, 'But Uncle Thomas said you lived in Holland?'

'I do, but I frequently work over here. When you are better I'd like to hear about your uncle.'

He picked up the tray and went to the door. 'Do as Emma tells you,' he warned and he left her.

She ate her breakfast presently and, although she had no intention of doing so, went sound asleep until Emma came back with a light lunch.

'Now I'll get up—I may, you know.'

'Yes, love. Just for a jiffy while I make your bed.'

'I'll stay up for tea,' said Matilda and walked on cotton-wool legs to the chair. It was barely a dozen steps away but she was absurdly glad to sit in it. When teatime came she was only too glad to get back into her bed.

It was a quiet house and the traffic in the street was infrequent. Once or twice she heard Dickens bark and twice footsteps going past her door. She drank her tea, took the pills Emma offered and went to sleep again.

She woke to find the doctor's face looming above her. A tide of self-pity engulfed her and for no reason at all she burst into tears.

He sat down on the bed and gathered her close, waiting patiently until she had sniffed and choked herself to a standstill, offered her a handkerchief, shook up her pillows and settled her against them.

Matilda drew a few shuddering breaths, aware that although she felt ill she no longer felt depressed. She pushed a cloud of hair away from her pale, red-eyed face and said in a watery voice, 'I'm sorry. I can't think why I did that. I'm quite all right now.'

'I did warn you,' he said cheerfully, 'but of course no one ever listens to the doctor in his own house.' He took his sopping handkerchief from her grasp and got up. 'I'm going to give you something to make you sleep soundly. Emma will bring you some soup presently and settle you for the night, and I promise you that in the morning you will feel almost your old self.'

'I can get up?'

'For an hour or so, but don't get dressed. I'll see you presently.'

He came back when she had eaten her soup and been washed and tidied to settle for the night. He watched her swallow the pills he gave her, wished her goodnight and went away again. She would have liked him to stay and talk, but he was in a dinner jacket ready to go out so she had said no more than goodnight. The pills were very effective; she had no time to do more than wonder where he was going and who with before she was asleep.

The doctor had been quite right; she felt quite her usual self when she woke in the morning, although she had the sense to know that if she got up and did too much she wouldn't feel too good. Emma brought her her tea and a visitor as well, Mrs Cribbs, a small mouselike woman with a gentle voice: the doctor's housekeeper.

'Me and Cribbs are so pleased that you're better, miss. You did have a nasty turn and no mistake.'

She slipped away, leaving Emma to explain that she and her husband ran the doctor's house for him. 'Not that he's here all that much—a week here and there and sometimes only a couple of nights—but it's handy for him to have a home to go to when he's finished with his lectures and such.'

She trotted round the room, setting it to right. 'In Vienna, 'e is, for a couple of days. Then back 'ere for a week before 'e goes back to Holland.'

Matilda sat up straight. 'But Emma, we can't stay here. He said we would discuss it and now he's gone away.'

'Yes, love, I was ter tell you that 'e'll talk about it when 'e gets back and you're not ter go out for a day or two, not until this east wind's stopped blowing.'

'He did, did he? He's being very bossy. Emma, we could go to your sister at Southend.'

'The wind'll be worse there,' said Emma. 'Now you have a nice warm bath and I'll bring up your breakfast.'

Matilda dressed after breakfast and went downstairs and was met by a portly middle-aged man who introduced himself as Cribbs, begged her to sit in the living-room and offered coffee. With the coffee came Mrs Cribbs. 'Maybe you'd like to see over the house, miss? The doctor said I was to ask you, just so you will know your way around.'

So Matilda passed a pleasant hour being shown the dining-room, very elegantly furnished in the Chippendale style, the pretty living-room, all pinky-beige and chestnut-brown and flowers everywhere, and the kitchen at the back of the house, which was a good deal larger than she had expected. There was another room on the ground floor; Mrs Cribbs opened the door and allowed her to peep in—the doctor's study, not to be entered unless invited. It was furnished with a large desk and a chair roomy enough to accommodate the doctor's vast frame and its walls were lined with books. The desk was littered with papers and books and Matilda had a strong urge to tidy it.

Upstairs there were three large bedrooms, besides her own, as well as two bathrooms. The main bedroom was at the back of the house with a small balcony overlooking the garden and its own bathroom and dressing-room. It was a beautiful room, all pale pastel colours with rosewood furniture and swathed brocade pelmets above the windows. Matilda sank her feet into the soft pile of the carpet. 'It looks ready to sleep in,' she observed.

'So it is, more or less, miss. I asked the doctor, very respectful, if he was thinking of marrying and he said, "Well, no, Mrs Cribbs, I can't say that I am at the moment, but it's as well to be ready, isn't it?" I dare say he's got some young lady in mind—Dutch, maybe?'

There was a small staircase leading to the floor above. 'Our flat,' explained Mrs Cribbs proudly. 'Me and Cribbs live here all the year round, caretaking as it were, seeing that everything is ready when the doctor comes—sometimes at a few hours' notice. Me and Cribbs are very happy here; we wouldn't work for anyone else but the doctor; a right good man he is.'

Emma echoed these sentiments later when she brought Matilda's lunch to the dining-room. When Matilda protested that she could quite well eat her meals in the kitchen with everyone else she was treated to a pained silence, followed by a brief homily from her old friend on the subject of knowing her place in the world and doing exactly what the doctor ordered. 'And that was that you was to have yer meals here or in the bedroom. And quite right, too.'

Matilda agreed meekly. It seemed a bit silly to her but presumably he had a reason for it and it was obvious that Emma had no intention of doing differently. She was more tired than she realised; it didn't take much persuasion on Emma's part for her to get on to her bed and snooze until teatime. After tea there was television to watch and the papers to read and a whole shelf of books to examine. She went happily to bed and had her supper on a tray, feeling a fraud but unable to deny that she was tired out.

She did better the next day. It was still cold outside and Emma wouldn't let her go out but there was plenty to do indoors. There was a small grand piano in the drawing-room, a vast apartment on a half-landing at the back of the hall which Matilda had found rather overpowering when she had been shown it by Mrs Cribbs, but, once inside, sitting at the piano, playing a little of this and that, she began to like the room. True, it was a bit splendid for her taste, but she supposed that if one had guests it would be a splendid background for party clothes; and there was a magnificent fireplace— Adam she thought, but she wasn't quite sure. While she was playing, Cribbs came in and put a match to the logs. She protested at that but he assured her gravely that the room was a good deal more pleasant with a fire burning. 'And the fire is always lighted when the room is occupied, miss.'

'I shouldn't have come, why didn't someone tell me? I'm sorry, Cribbs.'

He looked shocked. 'The doctor said that you were to

regard the house as your home, miss, and if I might say so it is a pleasure to have you with us.'

So Matilda spent the afternoon remembering odd snatches of music and enjoying every minute of it, and from time to time she got up and wandered round the room, looking at the portraits on the walls. The doctor must have had a vast number of ancestors, all rather stern, she decided. She preferred the landscapes and a group of delightful miniatures, ladies with smooth oval faces and ringlets, and one or two children's heads, too angelic to be true.

She had her tea and went back to the piano, her hands idling over the keys. It would be nice to see the doctor again, if only to thank him for his hospitality and bid him goodbye. She and Emma could go to a small hotel while she did a round of the agencies and got a job at one of the hospitals. She had some money, enough to keep them for a few weeks. Tomorrow, she promised herself, she would plan something so that when the doctor returned she would have a definite plan for her future. The thought unsettled her so she began another tour of the room, taking a second look at the paintings on its walls. One particular canvas was well worth another look: a group of a family with a stern-faced gentleman in its centre, a mid-Victorian from his dress, his hand on the back of the chair upon which his wife sat, a very pretty young woman in the lavish satins of that period, and presumably happy from the beaming smile upon her face. They were surrounded by children of various ages and a dog or two.

'You all look happy enough; I suppose Papa wasn't

as stern as he looks,' observed Matilda to the empty room.

Only it wasn't empty. Rauwerd van Kempler said, with the hint of a laugh, 'My great-great-grandfather, an eminent physician of his day, a devoted husband and a doting father. Great-great-grandmother was English; so for that matter is my grandmother.'

He stood there, smiling at her. 'You're better. Have you been bored?'

'Not in the least, thank you. I—I hope you don't mind; I've been playing the piano. I didn't know that you were coming back today.'

'Oh, I come and go,' he told her airily.

'Vienna, Emma said . . .'

The blue eyes stared down at her. 'Very wintry there.'

For some reason she felt vexed with him. She said austerely, 'I'm glad you're back Dr van Kempler. I am quite well again.' She drew a breath and embarked on the thank you speech she had thought over. 'I'm very grateful for your hospitality, it was very kind of you. I know you were Uncle Thomas's friend—I expect any friend would do the same . . .'

'Possibly. I must confess to having other reasons as well as that of a remembered friendship.'

She prided herself on her common sense. She said matter-of-factly, 'Oh, I expect you know of a job for me. I must confess that I'd hate to go back to that place, though I'm sorry for the old ladies.'

'There will be changes made; they will, I hope, have a much happier life. No, I don't know of a job for you, Matilda.' He strolled over to the fireplace and kicked a log into place, then turned to face her.

'I should like us to be married, and before you say anything, perhaps you will listen to me.'

He need not have said that; she was bereft of words. He studied her astonished face for a moment. 'You don't dislike me?'

She shook her head.

'Good, I am thirty-four, Matilda, I have a good practice with three partners, I travel a good deal, lecturing, examining, sitting on boards. I have a home in Holland and this house inherited from my grandmother. I have no financial worries, many friends and a busy life. I have for some time considered taking a wife—perhaps now that I am older I have a wish to come home to someone at the end of the day. I think that you might be that someone. I shall not insult your intelligence by saying that I love you. I have been in love—what man hasn't at my age?—but never loved, and there is a difference. I'm not in love with you, either. I like you enormously, I admire you, I enjoy your company, I believe that you will fit into my lifestyle and that I can make you happy, but I'm not prepared for any romance—we can have a working relationship and, I hope, a sound friendship. Perhaps later we can live as man and wife, but only if and when we both want that.' He smiled slowly. 'I've surprised you, but you're a sensible girl; think about it and let me know some time.' He glanced at his watch. 'I have to go out. I'm free tomorrow afternoon. Shall we go for a walk and talk about it?'

Matilda said slowly, 'I really don't know ...'

He said briskly, 'Of course you don't. You've not had

time to think about it, have you?' He crossed the room and put his hands on her shoulders and kissed her cheek gently. 'Till tomorrow, Matilda.'

She stood without moving after he had gone. He had called her a sensible girl; she only hoped that her senses would return to her in time for her to give him his answer on the following day. A refusal politely put.

CHAPTER FOUR

CONTRARY to her expectations, Matilda slept well and got up the next morning already composing a graceful refusal to the doctor's astonishing offer. She added to it, altered it, scrapped the whole thing and made up a new one before the day was half over. She had it off by heart by teatime and then forgot the whole thing when he walked into the drawing-room where she was curled up by the fire half asleep.

His hello was genial as he sat down in the chair on the opposite side of the fireplace. 'A little late for a walk, but we can talk here.'

She was struggling to remember the bare bones of what she had intended to say. 'There's really nothing to talk about,' she managed.

He chose to misunderstand her. 'Oh, good, I knew you'd be sensible.'

'I'm not being sensible,' she snapped. 'I really don't wish to marry you. It's—it's a preposterous idea; it couldn't possibly work . . .'

He settled back more comfortably into his chair. 'No? Tell me why not?'

The arguments she had marshalled all day so carefully melted away. She mumbled crossly, 'Well, I thought of a great many reasons.'

'All of them either romantic or illogical.' He smiled suddenly and she only just stopped herself in time from smiling back. 'Oh, they are real enough, but they hardly apply, do they? I'm not offering romance and all my reasons for marrying you are logical, aren't they?' He paused. 'Matilda, I wouldn't have proposed to you if I hadn't been certain that we could live together amicably.'

She said a little wildly. 'I want to marry for love.'

'I imagine that we all do. But love isn't always a flash of lightning; it can grow slowly from friendship and respect and regard.' He smiled again very kindly. 'Tell me, Matilda, did you—do you—love Leslie Waring?'

His voice was as kind as his smile and she paused to think so that she could give him an honest answer. 'Well, no—I sort of slipped into thinking that I did, if you see what I mean. We got on well and didn't quarrel and it would have been so nice for Uncle Thomas, and Mrs Waring seemed to like me.'

'None of them, if I might say so, good reasons for marrying.'

She said with a sudden flare of anger, 'Well, you tell me what they should be.'

'We will make an exception of love; that is a bonus in a happy marriage. Liking, respect, a shared interest in similar things, a similar background, an ability to laugh together and at each other, loyalty—they all add up to a happy marriage, even without your romantic ideas about falling in love—and that, my dear Matilda, isn't the same thing as loving. One can fall in love and out again—I'm sure we've both done that— but to fall in love and to love at the same time is, for those fortunate enough to do it, the crown of life.'

She eyed him in amazement. 'My goodness, you've given it some thought, haven't you?'

'Indeed I have.' His blue eyes gleamed. 'Logical thought.' When she didn't speak, he said, 'Will you marry me, Matilda? I believe that we may have a pleasant life together, even if unromantic. You will never be bored; I'm a busy man and I shall expect your help in many ways.' He smiled. 'Consider the alternatives and think about it. I've had a difficult day; I'll take a nap while you weigh up the pros and cons.'

He closed his eyes and there was no mistaking the fact that within a couple of minutes he was snoring very gently. Matilda sat and looked at him, thoughts running in all directions like frightened mice running from a cat. She called them to order and sensibly bent her reflections into a serious vein. He had, for him, had a lot to say and there was no doubt that it had been to the point. There had been no protestations of affection, let alone love; on the other hand, she felt certain that as long as she was a good wife he would be a good husband. He had harped on the unromantic aspect and she regretted that, for she was a romantic girl, and to marry a man who regarded her as a good friend and nothing more was lowering to say the least, but he was honest about it, and, she reminded herself, it wasn't as though she were in love with him. But she liked him ...

'Well?' asked the doctor without opening his eyes.

Of all the strange proposals, she thought pettishly and said coldly, 'I have a great many questions before I can even consider an answer.'

'Fire away.'

'Where would we live? What is to happen to Emma? Are you C of E? Do you have a family? Would you wish me to go on working after we are married?'

He raised a large, well-kept hand. 'Shall we deal with these first? I live in Leiden—there is a medical school there—in an old house with a quite nice garden. The town is old and charming and there is a good deal of social life. I have a wide circle of friends; they will be your friends, too. Emma, if she will, can make her home with us. I have a housekeeper who will be glad of help and the companionship of someone of her own age. Yes, I am the Dutch equivalent of C of E. My mother and father live near Hilversum, not too far away, and I have three sisters and two brothers. I'm the eldest. And, lastly, I most definitely do not wish you to continue working after we are married.'

'I haven't said ...' began Matilda.

'I am merely answering your questions, Matilda,' he told her smoothly.

She brooded for a moment on the alternatives life had to offer. A job at some hospital—the best she could hope for was a Staff Nurse's post while she caught up with modern methods and new drugs. A small flat with Emma to share it, enough money to live on, but only just, and the chance that she might meet someone who would want to marry her; not a very big chance, for she was, under her calm front, a shy girl and she had got out of the way of accepting the invitations of housemen because there was always Leslie. Besides, she had to admit to being a bit strait-laced, due no doubt to living with Uncle Thomas and Leslie's easy-going attitude; he had known her for years and any glamour in the relationship had long been rubbed off.

She drew a deep breath. 'All right, I'll marry you!' she said. 'I'm not sure if it's the right thing to do. If I were really honest I'd say no and find work and make a success of it, but if I marry you I'll do my best to be a good wife, only I do think you're getting the worst of the bargain.'

'Allow me to be the best judge of that, Matilda. Now, are we to settle on some plans for our marriage? Supposing we marry by special licence? Somewhere quiet—I'll make the arrangements if you agree to that. We can leave for Holland after the wedding. Have you any family you would like to have with you?'

She shook her head. 'No, Uncle Thomas was all I had.'

'Then shall we ask the rector to give you away? He was a friend of your uncle's, wasn't he?' He went on easily, 'I expect you want to buy clothes, and then it might be a good idea if you and Emma spent a few days with her sister at Southend. I'll be going to Manchester tomorrow for several days and if you feel up to it you could do your shopping. When I get back I'll drive you both down to Southend—the sea air will do you good.'

'For how long?' She felt that she was being rushed along towards a future she had hardly had time to contemplate.

'Oh, until a couple of days before the wedding. I shall be in Holland until then. My mother and father will want to come over to meet you; I think you will like them.'

He saw her rather blank look and added kindly, 'I'm rushing you along, aren't I? But there is really no point in waiting, is there? Do you suppose Emma will agree to come to Holland?'

'I think so; she hasn't anywhere to go here. My cousin only kept her because he was afraid of what people might say—she worked for Uncle Thomas for years and I don't think she ever expected to leave him.'

'Well, you talk to her, my dear. If she did dislike the idea we could find her a small flat near her sister and pension her off, but I think she'll want to stay with you.'

He got up and strolled across to the drinks set out on the sofa table. 'Will you have a sherry or do you prefer something else?'

He poured her drink and gave it to her. 'Have you enough money to buy all you need?' He sounded so matter-of-fact that she answered without hesitation, 'I think so, thank you. Uncle left me a little money—enough to get some clothes and something for Emma.' She added reflectively, 'It won't be a dressy affair, will it, our wedding?'

'Er, no, and you can get anything else you want when we get to Holland.'

She supposed that if they had been an ordinary couple, marrying for love and perfectly at ease with each other, they could have discussed little problems concerning money and what they would live on, but beyond the vague notion that the doctor appeared to be in comfortable circumstances she hadn't a clue as to his life and didn't like to ask.

He watched her, aware of her thoughts and smiling

a little. 'I shouldn't worry, Tilly,' he said quietly, 'we shall have plenty of time to discuss things later on—leave everything to me.'

Something she was only too glad to do.

She woke up the next morning to find Emma there with her early morning tea and the doctor leaning over the foot of the bed, watching her. His 'good morning' was genial and brisk. 'I'm just off,' he told her. 'I've fixed things with Emma's sister—Emma will tell you presently. Cribbs will drive you down in a couple of days; I won't be back. Take a taxi to the shops and back again and please don't overdo things.'

Matilda peered at him through her wealth of hair. 'Shan't I see you before you go to Holland?'

'It rather depends.' He didn't say on what. 'I'll keep in touch.'

He came round the bed and bent and kissed her cheek and was gone, leaving her indignant. 'Well, I never did!' she said explosively to Emma. 'Arranging everything like that without saying a word. I've a good mind to ...'

'Now, now, Miss Tilly,' said Emma placidly. 'No need to get worked up. You be glad that you're marrying a man who sees to everything for yer comfort. Proper gent, 'e is.' She trotted to the door. 'You drink your tea and after breakfast we'll do that shopping. Termorrer, too; I must have a new 'at.'

Matilda hopped out of bed and looked out of the window. The garden, rather bleak in the wintry morning, was empty. 'Where's Dickens?' she asked Emma's retreating back.

'Gorn with his master—very devoted 'e is. Always

lived 'ere with Mr Cribbs but the doctor says 'e's to go with us when we go to Holland. 'E says 'e won't be coming over quite so often when 'e's married.'

Matilda drank her tea and wondered why, but being a practical girl she didn't waste too much time about that but found paper and pencil and made a list of clothes. Most of her wardrobe was suitable for a GP's wife—and she supposed that he was a GP, with lecturing on the side, as it were—but she would have to have something to be married in: shoes, a couple of pretty dresses, more undies. She pruned the list to fit the contents of her balance at the bank, had a bath and dressed and, accompanied by Emma, got into the taxi Cribbs had waiting for them. Fenwick's would do, she had decided; pretty clothes, but not too wildly expensive.

It didn't take all that time to find what she wanted: palest pink crêpe and to go over it a darker, dimmer pink tweed coat. 'I need a hat,' she told the nice girl serving her. 'It's a wedding outfit,' and blushed when the girl's eyes slid to her left hand, looking for the ring which wasn't there.

The three of them went along to the hat department and found a velvet trifle which matched perfectly. 'You will look nice,' enthused the assistant. 'Your husband is going to like that.'

Matilda wondered if he would; he might not even notice what she was wearing. She put her gloves on over her ringless hand and paid the bill.

Emma, a country woman born and bred, didn't fancy any of the big stores. She settled for a majestic hat in plum-coloured felt which they found in a small shop off Oxford Street and, since they were both thirsty and a little tired, they had coffee before Matilda went in search of undies. It was almost lunchtime by then. She hailed a taxi and they went back to the doctor's house very pleased with themselves, already making plans to go again the next day.

She was getting into bed when the telephone on the bedside table rang. 'In bed?' asked the doctor.

'I was just getting in. We've had a lovely day shopping.'

'My name's Rauwerd. Have you finished your buying?'

'Not quite; we're going tomorrow morning.' She hesitated. 'Thank you for arranging everything, it was kind of you. Have you had a busy day?'

'Yes. You will be gone by the time I get back, but I'll find the time to come and see you in Southend before I go over to Holland. Sleep well, Tilly.' He rang off.

She found two pretty dresses the next day and, since there was still some money left, she bought a couple of sweaters and a silk blouse as well as a handbag and gloves for Emma. When they got back there was the packing to do. They wouldn't need much; she repacked almost all her things into her biggest suitcase and put it in the wardrobe, hung her wedding finery there as well, and declared herself ready to leave in the morning. Although she told herself that it didn't matter at all, she was decidedly disappointed when Rauwerd didn't telephone her.

They travelled to Southend in a Rover, a car, Cribbs told her, which was kept in London in case the doctor didn't drive himself over from Holland and which he and Mrs Cribbs were free to use when they wished. He was a chatty man, but Matilda couldn't get him to talk about his employer and after one or two discreet questions she gave up. She was a fool, she told herself worriedly, plunging head-first into matrimony. Indeed, by the time they had reached the end of their journey she was in a state of near panic. But that quickly subsided once she was in the company of Mrs Spencer and Emma; their matter-of-fact acceptance of the situation made it seem perfectly normal so that she ate her lunch, went for a brisk walk along the promenade before tea and went to bed directly after supper to sleep soundlessly.

The following evening the doctor telephoned. His calm voice dispersed any remnants of her doubts. He was going over to Holland on the following day, he told her, and he would be down in the morning to see her.

He hadn't said exactly when; Matilda was up betimes, ate a hasty breakfast and then mooned around, ignoring Emma's sensible observation that it was all of an hour's drive from London and it was still only nine o'clock.

Half an hour later he arrived, accepted the coffee Mrs Spencer offered him, passed the time of day with Emma and then suggested a walk with Matilda. 'I must leave at midday,' he said casually. 'I've still one or two things to see to.'

So Matilda got her coat and a scarf to tie round her head and they started off into the teeth of a strong cold wind. Presently he took her arm.

'I've settled everything for our wedding,' he told her. 'I shall be back in ten days' time and we shall marry two days later. I'll come for you and Emma—I'll let you know what time. Are you quite happy here, Tilly?'

'Oh, yes, thank you. Aren't you coming back before—we—we get married?'

'Probably I shall have to, but don't count on seeing me.' He stopped and turned her round so that the wind was at her back. 'I have something for you.' He put a hand into his pocket and took out a small box and opened it: a ring, a sapphire surrounded with diamonds set in gold. 'I hope it fits. It can be changed.'

It fitted. A good omen? Matilda took heart from that. She thanked him nicely but without gush, a little sad that they hadn't chosen it together.

'I should have liked to have had you with me,' said Rauwerd, unerringly reading her thoughts, 'but I tried to choose something we would both like.'

'It's beautiful, and I'm sure I'd have chosen it if we'd been together.'

He turned her round and they began to walk into the wind again. It wasn't possible to talk much; they turned back presently, blown along by the gale, and outside Mrs Spencer's house he flung a friendly arm around her. 'You look delightful.' And indeed she did, her eyes sparkling, her cheeks pink from their walk, and her hair whipped from its pins. He bent and kissed her cheek, the kiss of an old friend, nothing more. 'I'll not come in, I'm late already.' He opened the door and pushed her gently inside. '*Tot ziens*, Tilly.'

He had gone before she could answer.

She would ask him the next time they met what *Tot
ziens* meant. He had been casual about seeing her
again, but she had the rest of their life together to ask
him questions.

A week went by, Matilda, fully recovered from the
'flu, looked prettier than ever. She missed Uncle
Thomas, but that was a sorrow she kept to herself, and
already in those few weeks she had taught herself not
to think about her former home. The future mattered,
and she intended to make a success of it. The days
went by uneventfully, a kind of half-way house
between her past and her future. She read and knitted
and walked miles and gossiped gently with Emma and
her sister and thought about Rauwerd.

There were four days left before the wedding when
he came again, and then only briefly. He had returned
to fetch Dickens back to Holland, he told her, but he
would be back in two days' time and would drive
down to take her back to his house. He looked tired; all
the same he walked her along the esplanade in the
spring sunshine, not saying much, listening to her
quiet talk, and when he went after an hour or so he
said, 'You're a restful girl, Tilly—did anyone ever tell
you that?'

He gave her a casual kiss and got into his car and
drove off. It seemed to her that, pleasant though their
relationship was, it was unlikely to be more than that,
but she must never forget that she had been chosen by
him to be his wife; not for the usual reasons, it was
true, but it was satisfying to be wanted.

She and Emma were ready when he came to fetch
them two days later. It was still early and the road was

fairly empty so that the Rolls ate up the miles. They were almost at their journey's end when Rauwerd observed casually that his mother and father were at his home, a remark which had the effect of throwing her into a panic.

All to no purpose, as it turned out. At the end of the day, lying in her comfortable bed in the elegant room she had previously slept in, she mulled over the last few hours. Rauwerd's parents hadn't been at all what she had expected. They had been waiting in his drawing-room when they arrived, his father older than she had imagined, upright and as tall as his son, and his mother—she was tall, too; a fine figure of a woman, her uncle would have said—still good-looking in a severe way, although she had been kindness itself to Matilda. Thinking about it, Matilda decided that they liked her, just as she liked them; another good omen, she told herself.

They hadn't bothered her with a lot of questions, either, nor expressed the least surprise at their son's sudden decision to marry. Of course, he might have told them everything that was to be told, but somehow she doubted that. Tomorrow the best man and his wife would be arriving to lunch: a lifelong friend and his English wife. Matilda curled up in her bed and wondered what she should wear and she was still pleasantly occupied with this when she fell asleep.

Doubts as to whether the best man and his wife would like her rather clouded her morning, to be instantly dispelled when they arrived. Sybren Werdmer ter Sane was a large man, as large as the bridegroom. He engulfed Matilda's hand in his and twinkled down at her in a reassuring manner which put her at her ease, and as for his wife Rose—she was small and unassuming with magnificent brown eyes and a happy face. She was beautifully dressed, but then Sybren was an eminent surgeon in Amsterdam; she was also quite plainly the most important thing in her husband's life. Matilda suppressed a pang of envy as she led her upstairs to their room to tidy herself.

'Such fun,' said Rose. 'Rauwerd told us all about you, of course. He said you were very pretty and of course, you are. We shall be able to see each other— that's if you'd like to?' she added shyly.

'Oh, please. I don't know a thing about Holland or about Rauwerd's work. It'll be a bit strange ...'

'It's very like England and all the people you will meet speak English. Besides, Rauwerd will see that you have a good Dutch teacher.' Rose was sitting at her dressing-table, piling her mousy hair into a neat topknot. 'Sybren and Rauwerd were at Leiden together—he is little Sybren's godfather.'

'You've got a baby? How lovely! How old is he?'

'Six months and a bit. He's with his Granny and Grandpa and Nanny while we're here. He's gorgeous.' Rose patted the last strands into place and got up. 'Aren't you excited? We had a quiet wedding, too, but there was a huge party afterwards. Where are you going for your honeymoon?'

'Well, we have to go straight back to Leiden. I expect we'll go somewhere when Rauwerd's not so busy.' She gave Rose a bright smile. 'Let's go down if you're ready.'

Later that night, Rose, sitting up in bed watching

her husband emptying his pockets on to the dressing-chest, said thoughtfully, 'They don't seem very in love, darling; more like old friends who haven't seen each other for a long time. Do you think they will be happy?'

Her husband cast her a loving look. 'Yes, darling, I do. Perhaps not for a while, but neither of them are young and silly; they'll work at it and make a success of it. She is a nice girl and Rauwerd is one of the best.'

'Then why are they getting married?'

'I can think of a dozen reasons, all good.'

'When I know Matilda better, I shall ask her,' said Rose.

The sun shone in the morning, Matilda, getting into her wedding finery, peered out of the window and watched Rauwerd and Sybren strolling round the garden. From the back they looked rather alike in their sober grey suits and with their hair fair and silvery. Someone called them from the house and Matilda withdrew her head smartly, but not before Rauwerd had seen her and given her a casual wave.

They were to be married at a small church a bare five minutes' drive away. Matilda, waiting nervously in the drawing-room with the rector after everyone else had gone, swallowed down panic behind a calm face. There had been no time for that until now; when she had gone downstairs to meet the others there had been a good deal of cheerful talk and her future mother-in-law had taken a velvet case from her handbag and begged her to open it.

'All the wives have it in turn, and now it's for you,

Matilda, my dear,' she had said kindly. 'Will you wear it?'

A brooch, rose diamonds, any number of them in an old-fashioned setting of gold. It sparkled and shone and Mevrouw van Kempler said gently, 'Let me put it on for you, dear, and wish you all the happiness in the world.'

Rose had given her a present, too, to be opened later, she whispered, and so had the rector. Emma's present was packed: a dozen of the finest lawn hankies, housed in a quilted sachet which had been her sister's gift. There had been nothing from the Warings or her aunt and Herbert. Rauwerd had put the notice of their marriage in the *Telegraph* and she had hoped that they might have sent a card. It was a little frightening not to have family or friends; perhaps, she thought hopefully, she would find both in Holland.

She followed the rector out to the car and, when they arrived at the church, walked steadily beside him up the aisle to where Rauwerd was waiting.

She walked just as steadily down the aisle, her arm tucked into Rauwerd's, twenty minutes later. The plain gold ring on her finger proclaimed her to be married but she didn't feel any different. Indeed, she was suddenly very scared. Perhaps Rauwerd guessed what she felt, for he gave her hand a gentle reassuring squeeze and, when she looked at him, smiled at her with an equally gentle smile, so kind that she felt tears pricking her eyes. She wasn't scared any more; everything would be all right. She liked him now, even if she hadn't when they had first met, and she respected him, and that was surely more important between husband and wife? She smiled back at him and got into the Rolls beside him and was driven back to her new home.

There was a luncheon party, of course. Mrs Cribbs had excelled herself with lobster patties, caviare, tiny sausages on sticks, chicken vol-au-vents and smoked trout, followed by *crêpes de volaille florentine*, a variety of salads and *asperges polonaise*, and finally the wedding cake, cut with due ceremony and washed down with champagne. Presently it was time for Matilda to change into a jersey dress to wear under the new tweed coat and to pack the last of her things. She was taking a final critical look at herself when there was a tap on the door.

'Ready?' asked Rauwerd. 'You do look nice, Tilly. They are all waiting to say goodbye.'

She collected her gloves and handbag and went downstairs with him, feeling shy, to be instantly engulfed in a round of embracing and kissing.

'We shall see you very soon, my dear,' Rauwerd's mother told her. 'We travel back tomorrow.' His father hugged her close and kissed her cheek. 'I couldn't have chosen a lovelier bride myself,' he told her gallantly.

Rose and Sybren were staying for a few days and going to fly back. 'I'll give you a ring as soon as we get home,' promised Rose and stood back to allow Emma to say goodbye. Not for long, for she was to travel to Holland with Rose and Sybren.

'Just you be 'appy, the pair of yer,' whispered Emma.

They drove to Dover and went by hovercraft over to Calais. It was all new to Matilda. The Rolls ate up the two hundred-odd miles they had to go, along the coast to Bruges, skirting Antwerp, and then on to Breda, stopping for tea before they reached Dordrecht. Here Rauwerd left the motorways, taking a route which took them to Schoonhoven, Gouda, and then, avoiding Alpen aan de Rijn, Boskoop and finally Leiden.

Rauwerd had bypassed the towns and cities, so that Matilda had her first real glimpse of an old Dutch town as he slowed to go into its centre.

She had been careful not to chatter, but now she exclaimed, 'Oh, look—all those old houses and the gables, and what is that little castle built up on that mound?'

'That is the Burcht—eleventh century, with a fort overlooking the old and new Rhine. We're turning off here, before we reach it. This is the Rapenburg Canal; the university and the museums and laboratories are here.' After a moment he added, 'And this is where our home is.'

She could have hugged him for that 'our'.

He turned the Rolls into a narrow street lined with tall old houses, three and four storeys high, their massive front doors reached by double stone steps guarded by wrought iron palings. He stopped at the first house, its high stone wall abutting on to Rapenburg, its elegant front facing the tree-lined street.

Rauwerd got out and came round the bonnet to open Matilda's door. He took her hand and went with her up the steps to where a stout elderly man was waiting at the open door. Rauwerd said something to him in Dutch and added, 'Matilda, this is Jan. He has been in the family for a very long time and looks after me; he will be only too delighted to look after you as well. His wife does the housekeeping; her name is Bep.'

Jan bent his portly frame in a bow. 'Welcome, Mevrouw—we are delighted.'

His English was heavily accented but it cheered her enormously. She shook hands and, urged by Rauwerd, went into the house. The hall was lofty and narrow, the ceiling hung with pendant bosses, the walls panelled in some dark silk and hung with oil paintings. There was a marble-topped console table against one wall and a long case clock with floral marquetry on the opposite wall; the floor was black and white tiles. Exactly like an old Dutch interior on a museum wall, thought Matilda, as she allowed herself to be led forward to where Bep was waiting, small and stout as her husband and with just as warm a welcome. Rauwerd said something to her and she smiled and slipped through a door at the back of the hall while Jan opened the double doors facing the clock. The room was long and wide and as lofty as the hall. The windows overlooking the street were draped in a rich plum-coloured velvet with elaborate pelmets, a colour repeated in the brocade of the chairs and sofas each side of the hearth. A lovely room, with a magnificent plaster ceiling, the walls lined with glass-fronted display cabinets.

Rauwerd, standing beside her, watched her face as

she turned to him, to be interrupted by the re-opening
of the door and the entry of Dickens. He was a well-
behaved dog but his greeting was none the less
ebullient. By the time they had made much of him,
Bep was back, waiting to take Matilda to her room.
But before she went Rauwerd caught her by the hand.

'Welcome to our home, Tilly,' he said and bent and
kissed her cheek.

She stared up at his quiet face. 'It is a very beautiful
one,' she told him seriously. 'We'll be happy here.'

There was a faintly anxious question in her voice
and he said at once, 'Of course we shall.' He smiled
reassuringly. 'Don't be too long; Bep has a meal ready
for us.'

CHAPTER FIVE

THE staircase was at right angles to the hall, its oak treads curving round to the narrow gallery above. The gallery had several doors leading from it and a corridor leading to the back of the house, which hadn't looked large from the outside; but now that she was inside, Matilda came to the conclusion that she had been mistaken about that. The doors were mahogany crowned by carved wreaths of fruit and flowers. Bep opened one of them and ushered Matilda into a large room at the front of the house.

The furniture was of yew, the bedhead beautifully decorated with marquetry to match the sofa-table between the tall windows, and the tallboy against one of its walls. There was a thick carpet underfoot and the long curtains of old-rose matched the bedspread. A magnificent room, with its enamelled wall sconces, the gilded triple mirror on the sofa-table and the two small easy chairs on either side of a lamp-table. Just right for a midnight gossip, thought Matilda, and stifled a giggle at the very idea. The giggle had been nervous; she called upon her common sense and followed Bep across the room to the door in the far wall. A bathroom, fitted with every conceivable luxury, and leading to another room. This would be Rauwerd's she guessed: a little austere, its windows at the side of the house overlooking the Rapenburg Canal. There was a door in that

room, too; she opened it and peeped out. The gallery
led to a narrow passage with more doors; it would take
her a month of Sundays to find her way around. She
went back to her bedroom and, when Bep left her, did
her face and hair and presently went downstairs.

Rauwerd was sitting on the bottom stair, reading a
newspaper. He got up as she reached him and smiled at
her. 'Over here,' he said. 'It's a funny old house but
you'll soon find your way around.'

The dining-room was on the opposite side of the hall,
with windows overlooking the street as well as the
Rapenburg. It wasn't as large as the drawing-room and
was furnished in the rather heavy Beidermeier style.
But somehow it suited the room, with its patterned
crimson wallpaper and matching curtains. The table
was oval and the cloth upon it was starched linen, set
with heavy silver and sparkling glass. There was a
beautiful old Delft bowl full of hyacinths at its centre
and crystal wall sconces shed light on it.

'You have a very beautiful home here,' said Matilda,
doing her best not to sound overawed.

'I'm glad you like it, Tilly. It's very old, as you can
see, and I'm told the very devil to keep clean, but I love
it. If you are not too tired, we'll go on a tour of
inspection presently.'

Their dinner was delicious, although, thinking
about it later, Matilda wasn't at all sure what they ate.
Certainly they had drunk champagne, so that by the
time they started on their tour of the house, she was
feeling decidedly cock-a-hoop.

They wandered slowly from room to room. There
was a small sitting-room behind the drawing-room,

opening on to a veranda leading to the garden, which was long and narrow and walled with rose-coloured bricks. Back in the house, she was allowed to peep into the study before going upstairs.

'Bep will show you the kitchen,' explained Rauwerd. 'She and Jan will be having their supper.' He paused on the gallery. 'You've seen your own room, of course, and the bathroom. My room's beyond that. There are two more rooms on that side, with a bathroom and two rooms opposite.'

He led her round, waiting patiently while she paused before a picture or admired the furniture, and then climbed another staircase tucked away at the end of a short passage. 'Bep and Jan have their flat there.'

There was a door at the head of the staircase and he opened it to reveal a short passage with a door on either side. 'They're here.' He waved an arm. 'Emma shall have the room on this side.' He opened the door and showed her a large room, nicely furnished. 'There's a bathroom through there and I expect you and Bep can contrive to make everything comfortable for her.'

'She'll love it,' declared Matilda. They were in the back passage. 'What's that?'

A narrow steep staircase at the end. 'The attics—two of them. We loved them when we were children.' He added abruptly, 'If you've seen all you want to, shall we go down again? Is there anything you want before you go to bed?'

She felt a pang of disappointment; she would have liked to have sat down quietly somewhere and talked. She said composedly, 'Nothing, thank you. It's been a long day, hasn't it?'

She skipped down in front of him and when they reached the gallery opened her door. She gave him a bright smile and asked cheerfully, 'What time is breakfast?'

'Half-past seven, but you can have it when you like.'

She kept the smile there. 'I'm used to getting up early. Goodnight, Rauwerd.'

Not a very good start, she reflected as she got to bed, but perhaps they were both feeling awkward. Not that she could imagine Rauwerd feeling awkward for any reason at all. Perhaps he was regretting their marriage already. She dismissed the idea as silly. She was tired; it had indeed been a long day—her wedding day.

In the morning everything was all right. Somehow, sitting opposite him, eating breakfast together, it seemed as though they had been doing just that for years; not talking much but content with each other's company. Indeed, from Rauwerd's manner, they might have been married a decade at least.

She debated within herself as to whether that was a good thing or not. It would certainly make for a placid, undemanding relationship; on the other hand it would be nice to stir up a little interest. Nothing much, just enough for him to look at her twice.

She was roused from her thoughts by Rauwerd's pleasant voice. 'You are very far away, Tilly . . .' There was a faint question there and hastily she assured him that she had merely been wool gathering.

'There is such a lot to think about—it's rather like a dream.'

'Let us hope that the reality will be as nice. I have to go to the hospital this morning and I have some patients to see this afternoon; I won't be home for lunch. Will you be happy here? Bep's longing to take you all over the house again and I dare say you want to unpack. I should be home by four o'clock or thereabouts and perhaps we can discuss several matters.'

'What matters?'

'Oh, lessons—for you. The quicker you learn to speak Dutch the better. You can drive? Good, then you must have a car. Now that I have a wife we can entertain from time to time, and there are various functions at the hospital and medical school you will attend with me, so you'll need clothes.'

He got up and paused by her chair. 'It's all strange for you, isn't it? But you're sensible and you will soon have friends.'

'And you,' said Matilda rather tartly.

'Yes, yes, of course. I have no doubt that we shall settle down very well together.'

He laid a hand on her shoulder for a moment. 'I must be off.'

She sat for some minutes after he had gone, frowning, considering what he had said. Perhaps it would be best to wait until he came home; it would be nice to know something more about their social life. In the meantime she would try and learn something of her wifely duties.

Bep was delighted to show her the contents of the linen cupboards, the china pantry and the baize-lined drawers containing the table silver. The morning passed in a flash and after lunch Matilda toured the garden with Dickens. It wasn't large, but it had been laid out with imagination and she spent an hour poring over labels and poking her nose around the beds. She went indoors presently and sat by the fire with the dog beside her while she tried to make out the headlines of the newspapers. She was engrossed in this when Rauwerd got home.

He paused in the doorway, for she made a charming picture curled up in an armchair by the hearth with Dickens pressed close to her, and with her pretty nose buried in the paper. Dickens rushed to meet him and she folded the paper neatly and got up. 'I'll ask Bep for tea,' she said and smiled a little shyly.

'I saw Jan as I came in; he's bringing it now. Have you been bored?'

He sat down opposite her and Dickens lay at his feet.

'Bored? Heavens, no. Bep showed me everything—you know, the linen and the silver and the kitchen. And after lunch Dickens and I went into the garden and I've been trying to read the newspaper ever since.'

'I'm very sorry I wasn't free to spend the day with you. My partners and their wives have invited us to dinner—they want to celebrate our wedding—and I accepted for us both. In two days' time. I expect you may like to get a new dress for the occasion? Which reminds me—I've opened an account for you at my bank and paid in your quarter's allowance. Let me know if you run out of money.'

Jan came in with the tea and he sat silent while she poured it out but presently she said, 'Thank you, Rauwerd. Yes, I'll need a dress, I think. Are they very smart your partners' wives?'

'Nicely dressed,' he observed. 'They are easy to get on with. Jacob Thenus and Beatrix—he's the senior of

the three—they have three children. Then there is
Pieter van Storr and Marie—they have a boy and a girl,
then Gus and Gerda Swijstra—he joined us two years
ago. The dinner is to be held at Jacob's house in Leiden
and they are all looking forward to meeting you. But
don't worry about not speaking Dutch, they all speak
English.'

He passed his cup for more tea. 'If you would like it, I
will arrange for you to start Dutch lessons with a retired
Professor of English; he's elderly but a splendid
teacher. He lives on the other side of the canal and
perhaps you would like to go to his house. He's rather
crippled with arthritis and he doesn't get around
much.'

'I'd like that. Will it take me long to learn Dutch?'

He reassured her. 'No, you're an intelligent girl and
besides you will have the day-to-day running of the
household and the shopping, which will be excellent
practice for you.' He put his cup down and got to his
feet. 'I must do some work and take Dickens for his
walk. I'll see you at dinner, my dear.'

He strolled to the door. 'By the way, I've ordered a
car for you.'

She should have been delighted; instead she felt
forlorn. A walk with Dickens would have been very
pleasant, and they could have talked. But he didn't
seem to want her company, although he was kind and
considerate and generous. Perhaps it would be better
once he had got used to having a wife.

She went shopping for a dress the next day. There
were some delightful boutiques in Leiden and she spent
some time searching for what she wanted. She found it

finally: amber crêpe, finely pleated and deceptively simple. It took almost all the money she had but it would be, she decided, just right.

Rauwerd came home to lunch, and they talked about nothing much until he asked, 'Did you go shopping?'

'Yes. I found a dress, too. There are some nice shops ...'

'Let me know if you run out of money.'

'Well, I haven't used any of yours yet. I had a little of my own.'

He said evenly, 'You are my wife, Matilda. I expect you to use the allowance I have arranged for you.' He glanced at the clock. 'I must go. Private patients until five o'clock. I've sent Emma her ticket—she will be coming next week. We'll meet her, shall we?'

He laid a large hand on her shoulder and went to the door. 'I'll not be back until some time after six o'clock.'

Matilda dreaded the dinner party. She was dressed far too early; Rauwerd was just arriving when she went downstairs. If she had but known, she had never looked lovelier; the rich colour of the dress suited her and apprehension had lent colour to her cheeks and a sparkle to her eyes. Rauwerd, pausing in the doorway, took a long look at her. 'Charming,' he said softly. 'I'll be fifteen minutes.'

He came down presently, wearing another of his sober, beautifully cut suits and helped her into her coat and then put his hand in a pocket.

'I almost forgot. You must forgive me, my dear.' He fastened a choker of pearls around her neck. 'A belated wedding gift.'

She put up a hand to feel their creamy smoothness.

'Thank you, Rauwerd.'

And was quite nonplussed when he added, 'They've been in the family for a very long time.'

Her dread had been unnecessary; Jacob Thenus and his wife were ready to welcome her with open arms. Jacob was thickset, with a round face, bright eyes and an endearing smile, and Beatrix was a small fairylike creature, who kissed Matilda with warmth. 'Isn't it nice,' she observed, 'now we're all married? Come and meet the others.'

Pieter van Storr and Marie were a little older, tall and strongly built and just as warm in their greeting, and Gus and Gerda Swijstra were a young and lively couple whom she liked at once.

Jacob lived in Leiden, too, in an old house on the outskirts of the town, and he and Beatrix had gone to a good deal of trouble to make a success of their dinner party. And it was a success. Matilda, watching Rauwerd, saw that he was on excellent terms with his partners, an observation borne out by Gerda as they chatted over drinks.

'He is nice, your Rauwerd,' she said. 'He is the boss, but we're all friends. We are so happy that he is married, now we shall no longer have to find pretty girls for him when there is a party. He has found his own for himself.' She beamed at Matilda. 'You find it all a little strange, I expect, but not for long. Leiden is a most friendly part and there is much to do.'

Someone had gone to a lot of trouble over dinner: lobster soup, morsels of fish in a delicious sauce, champagne sorbets and beef tournedos, followed by a magnificent dessert which, Beatrix explained, had been made especially in honour of the newly married pair. There was champagne, too, and speeches and a great deal of laughing and cheerful talk. Matilda went to bed that night feeling that she had made some friends, and the thought was comforting.

What was even more comforting was Rauwerd's suggestion that, since he could spare an hour or so on the following morning, they might go to den Haag and do some shopping. 'For you will get asked out to coffee and tea,' he told her, 'as well as dinner parties to which we shall be invited.'

Before they set out the next day he gave her a cheque book. 'And if you find yourself short of money just ask to have whatever it is charged to me,' he told her casually.

'Are you very rich?' asked Matilda.

'Well, yes.' He smiled down at her. 'But let us go and make me a little poorer, shall we?'

She had a heavenly time. Rauwerd took her to Lange Voorhout and Noordeinde and waited with patience while she shopped. The sum he had mentioned as her quarterly allowance had left her open-mouthed, but the desire to spend was irresistible. She wasn't a foolish spender but she had the sense to know that she was quite inadequately dressed as the wife of an eminent and wealthy doctor. She didn't dither; she knew what she needed and bought it while Rauwerd sat quietly in a number of boutiques and nodded his approval. When at length she professed herself satisfied he bore her off to tea and rich cream cakes at a teashop in Lange Voorhout and, as they left, observed regretfully that he would be out that evening.

'You won't mind dining alone?' he asked. 'I shall be very late in.'

She assured him that she didn't mind at all and wondered silently what could possibly occupy him at the hospital so late in the day. Although they had been on excellent terms all the day she couldn't bring herself to ask.

Back at the house he unloaded all her parcels and band boxes. 'I'll see you at breakfast,' he observed casually. 'Goodnight, Tilly.'

'A lovely day,' she told herself, going up to her room, stifling loneliness; and to pass the time before dinner, she tried on all her new clothes.

She went to bed soon after dinner, for the house seemed very silent. Dickens had gone with Rauwerd, and Jan and Bep, after making sure that she lacked for nothing, had retired to the kitchen to their own supper. She had a bath, lying in the hot water, reading until the water cooled, and at last getting into bed, to lie awake until she heard Rauwerd's quiet footfall just before midnight.

At breakfast she asked, 'Were you very busy at the hospital last night?'

He gave her a cool stare. 'I wasn't at the hospital, Matilda. Would you like to visit my parents this weekend? We could go over on Sunday morning for coffee. I have to go out after lunch so we had better have it here. I'm free on Saturday; if you care to we'll drive around so that you can see something of Holland.'

She thanked him nicely and wondered where he was going on Sunday afternoon. She was behaving like a suspicious wife, she reflected.

She was too sensible to waste time on idle conjecture. She found plenty to occupy her during the following day and on Saturday morning, dressed in one of the new outfits—a pleasing speckled tweed suit—went down to breakfast anticipating a very pleasant day.

So it was. Rauwerd drove her north to the Frisian Lakes, gave her coffee in Sneek, allowed her half an hour in which to glimpse the little town, then went on to Leeuwarden and north to the coast of Groningen. Here they lunched off enormous pancakes at Nenkemaborg Castle, after exploring its interior. They returned along country roads, narrow and often built in brick, but affording Matilda a good look at rural Holland. They stopped for tea at a small wayside café and then drove home through an early evening grown suddenly gloomy.

The weather might be depressing but Matilda hadn't felt so happy for a long time. Rauwerd, who had seemed so remote, revealed himself to be an amusing companion, easy to talk to and willing to answer her endless questions. She got out of the car with regret; the day had gone too quickly and now she supposed Rauwerd would go to his study . . .

He joined her in the hall as Jan shut the street door. 'You've had a dull time for a bride, Matilda. Shall we go out to dinner and dance afterwards?'

She beamed her delight. 'Oh, Rauwerd, how lovely. I'd like that.' She frowned. 'But I ordered dinner . . .'

He glanced at his watch. 'I doubt if Bep has started on it yet.' He spoke to Jan who smiled and nodded and went away in the direction of the kitchen. 'Wear that pink dress you bought the other day.'

He took her to den Haag, to the Saur Restaurant, where they dined off lobster thermidor and drank champagne, and later he drove to Scheveningen and they danced. He danced well with casual perfection, saying little, and Matilda was content that he did. The evening was proving a delight and she didn't want it to end; indeed, it was the small hours before they returned home.

'A lovely evening, Rauwerd,' she told him as they went indoors. 'Thank you ...' She would have said more but his coolly polite, 'I'm glad you enjoyed it, Matilda,' took the words from her. She wished him a quiet goodnight and went to bed, vaguely unhappy, and not quite sure why.

He was his usual calm and friendly self at breakfast and during the drive to Hilversum. The elder van Kemplers lived in a square house with a steep roof, painted white and with green shutters to its windows. It stood in a large garden beautifully landscaped, a mile or so outside one of the many villages around the town.

'Have your family always lived here?' asked Matilda.

'Yes. A van Kempler built it early in the eighteenth century, and its been added to and modernised from time to time. You like it?'

'It looks charming.' She got out of the car feeling nervous. His family had been kind to her on their wedding day but they might have had second thoughts since then.

They hadn't. She was welcomed warmly, swept into a vast drawing-room and plied with coffee and small crisp biscuits while Mevrouw van Kempler chatted about nothing much. But presently she began to talk about the family: Rauwerd, the eldest ...

'Six children,' she observed contentedly. 'The other boys are away—they'll be home shortly; both married, as are his sisters. Rauwerd has taken longer than the others to find himself a bride.' She beamed at Matilda and patted her hand. 'And such a dear girl, too. His father and I are so pleased, my dear. He works so hard, he needs a wife and children to slow him down a little.'

Matilda murmured and to her own annoyance blushed, something which Mevrouw van Kempler noted with pleasure.

It was too chilly a day to go into the garden; Matilda was taken on a tour of the vast conservatory at the back of the house instead, walking with her father-in-law, able, to her relief, to carry on quite a sensible conversation about the variety of plants growing there. She liked the elderly man, so like his eldest son, yet so much easier to talk to.

Before they left, Rauwerd, sitting with his mother, called across to her, 'My dear, we would like Mother and Father to come to dinner one evening, wouldn't we? I'm free on Thursday after lunch, shall it be then?'

His manner towards her made her feel very married. She agreed smilingly and hoped that his parents wouldn't guess at the real state of affairs, for she liked them too much to hurt them.

They went back home for lunch and soon afterwards Rauwerd left home saying that he hoped to be back for dinner but he would ring her if he found it impossible.

She almost bit her tongue off in her efforts not to ask him where he was going. She said serenely, 'Very well, Rauwerd,' and returned his intent look with a smile, aware that he was expecting her to question him.

Dickens didn't go with him. Matilda spent the evening watching a television programme she couldn't understand, then walked Dickens in the garden. When Rauwerd phoned, as she had guessed he would, she assured him that she was having a pleasant evening, had her dinner and went to bed very early.

Not, however, to sleep; not until long after midnight when she heard the car and presently Rauwerd's quiet footsteps going past her door.

She forbore, with the greatest effort, from mentioning the previous evening over their breakfast, but remarked brightly that it was a fine morning and she intended to explore the town.

He would be home for lunch, he told her, and would she phone Rose and ask her and Sybren for dinner on Thursday? 'They are friends of my parents. I have to go to Amsterdam on Friday—I should like to bring back an old friend to dinner; we'll need someone to make a fourth, and I'll ask Professor Vouters—I was his registrar years ago and we've not lost touch, although he's retired now. You'll like him.'

It was only after he had gone that Matilda remembered that he hadn't said anything about the old friend in Amsterdam.

She had a long talk with Rose on the phone. They were going to be friends, she felt sure of that, and Rose's sensible reassurances about the pitfalls Matilda was likely to encounter made life seem suddenly rather fun.

'Little Sybren's cut a tooth,' said Rose. 'We're so pleased with him. Wait till you have a baby; they're such fun. What are you going to wear on Thursday?'

Matilda went to see Bep in the kitchen and, with Jan to translate, discussed the dinner parties. It took the best part of half an hour to decide on the two menus and at the end of it, Bep asked her if she would buy flowers for the house.

The florists were bursting with early spring flowers as well as great bunches of hothouse roses and carnations. She bore a great armful back to the house and spent the rest of the morning happily arranging them. Setting the last vase just so in the drawing-room, she felt a pleasant little glow; she was beginning to feel like a housewife. Once she had mastered sufficient Dutch she would be able to order the groceries and see the butcher and the greengrocer and inspect the cupboards . . . and Emma would arrive on Sunday. She told herself that she didn't feel lonely or strange any more. Which wasn't quite true.

She was nervous about the dinner parties but she need not have been, at least for the first one. No one could have been kinder than Rauwerd's mother and father, and Rose and Sybren treated her with the ease of long friendship, even though they hardly knew her. The evening was a success; she wore a patterned crêpe dress and the pearl choker, and the dinner was excellent. Listening to Rauwerd laughing and talking with Sybren and his father, she found herself wishing that he could talk and laugh like that with her. He treated her with charming manners and thoughtfulness but with a reserve which made an invisible barrier between them. Something which would improve with time, she told herself.

'A penny for them?' said Rose.

'It's all a bit strange,' began Matilda.

'Don't let it get you down. I spent the first few weeks wondering if I should have married Sybren or not even though I'm crazy about him. It's just getting used to them being important and horribly rich and quite sure of themselves. Don't worry, it won't last. Sybren's the most modest of men when it comes to his fame, and Rauwerd's the same. They take money for granted, and being venerated by students and all that.' She beamed at Matilda. 'I'm so happy, I can't believe it. You are, too, only all this——' she waved a hand round the lovely room '——takes a bit of getting used to. You're coming to dine with us as soon as we can fix a date. Rauwerd has to go to Brussels this week, hasn't he? So it'll have to be the week after.'

Mevrouw van Kempler joined them then, which saved Matilda answering.

Confident that the second dinner party would be as successful as the first one, Matilda put the finishing touches to the table, put on another new dress, silvery green this time with long tight sleeves and a round low neckline which set off the pearls to perfection. Going down to the drawing-room in her new kid slippers, she felt a surge of confidence as she opened the drawing-room door.

Rauwerd was there, sitting in his chair, laughing at something the woman sitting in her chair opposite had said. He got up as she paused in the doorway, and said easily, 'Ah, my dear, there you are. We got here earlier than we had expected. This is Nikky van Wijk, who lives in Amsterdam.'

The woman had got up and he touched her on the arm. 'Nikky, my wife, Matilda.'

She wasn't very young—mid-thirties perhaps—but she was strikingly handsome with silver-blonde hair, cool blue eyes and regular features. She smiled charmingly as she took Matilda's hand, but her eyes didn't smile.

Matilda disliked her on sight.

'I'll leave you to get to know each other,' said Rauwerd smoothly, 'while I change.'

'You've known Rauwerd a long time?' asked Nikky, still smiling.

'Not long,' said Matilda politely.

Nikky waited for her to say something else and, when she didn't, observed, 'We've known each other for years, but of course you know that already. It's nice of you not to mind that he's spent so much time with me.' She shrugged prettily. 'I'm a fool over business. I don't know what I'd do without Rauwerd to help me—and we have so much to talk about.'

'I expect so; you're much the same age, are you not?' Matilda, by no means a catty girl, sharpened her claws.

The blue eyes became very cold indeed. 'Rauwerd is thirty-three ...'

'Thirty-four,' corrected Matilda gently.

'I'm a good deal younger,' began Nikky and was interrupted by Rauwerd's return. Hard on his heels came Professor Vouters, a dear old man she took an instant liking to. The conversation became general over their drinks and presently they went in to have dinner: clear asparagus soup, crayfish in a rich cream sauce flavoured with anchovy, a lemon sorbet before the pork fillets cooked in a madeira sauce and finally a fresh fruit salad and whipped cream.

Professor Vouters sat back with a sigh. 'A delicious meal, Matilda—I may call you that? Rauwerd has chosen himself an excellent wife and a very beautiful one.' He raised his glass to her. 'You and I must become friends. You must have time to spare while Rauwerd works, and I, alas, have more time on my hands than I would wish. You must come and visit me and I will show you our famous Hortus Botanicus gardens. There are also a number of museums, but perhaps you do not care for those?'

He sounded so wistful that she assured him that she did.

They talked over their coffee and presently Professor Vouters got up to go. It seemed that he lived very close by; all the same as Matilda wished him goodnight a silent Jan appeared to escort him into the street and the few hundred yards to his flat.

'He must be eighty,' remarked Nikky lightly from her seat by the fire. 'Time he went into a home.'

Matilda was pleased to see the look of annoyance on Rauwerd's face. 'Certainly not! His brain is as clear as yours or mine—clearer, probably.'

'I forgot that he was one of your fans, Rauwerd!' She sat up gracefully. 'I've had a lovely evening, but I should get back.' She smiled at Matilda. 'You don't mind if Rauwerd runs me home? Silly little me can't drive a car.'

She turned to Rauwerd. 'And while you are there, will you spare five minutes to look over that tiresome paper I had from the *notaris*?'

'A little late,' observed Rauwerd blandly.

'Not really. Good gracious, we've been up later than this before now. And it will save you coming tomorrow—you'll be going to Brussels . . .'

Just as though I weren't here, fumed Matilda silently, and smiled a little too brightly. Matters were getting out of hand; a little talk might clear the air—that was, she thought sourly, if he could spare the time between seeing to Nikky's affairs and going to Brussels!

She bade her guest goodnight in a serene voice and expressed the hope that they might meet again very soon, aware that Rauwerd was looking at her in his disconcertingly direct way. She bade him goodnight, too, and wished she hadn't when she saw Nikky's nasty little smile.

Perhaps, being such an old friend, Nikky knew all about their marriage. She dismissed the thought as unworthy of Rauwerd.

It was absurd to imagine that she was jealous. All the same, she lay awake until she heard the car return.

At breakfast Rauwerd told her that he would be in Brussels for the whole of the day. 'I should get back in the evening,' he told her, 'but don't wait dinner for me.'

She said coldly, 'Yes, Rose and your friend Nikky told me that you would be there. Would you like a meal left for you?'

'Coffee, perhaps, and some sandwiches.' He added silkily, 'I should have told you, but I'm not used to having a wife.'

Matilda buttered a roll. 'No. Emma gets here tomorrow, doesn't she?'

'I hadn't forgotten. We'll meet her at Schiphol. The plane gets in at five o'clock.'

He gathered up his post and got to his feet. 'I'll be home about ten o'clock.' He stood looking at her. 'Months ago I accepted an invitation to a seminar in Las Palmas. Would you like to go with me? I could manage a week's holiday added on to the week's seminar.'

He strolled to the door. 'Think about it,' he suggested, 'and let me know this evening.'

She could have told him then and there. Of course she would go, and not just because it would be marvellous to spend two weeks in the sun. Las Palmas was a long way from Leiden; it was also a long way from Amsterdam and Nikky.

CHAPTER SIX

MATILDA began her morning's routine: the flowers, shopping with Bep at her elbow to help with the difficult bits and then a walk with Dickens who, of course, had had to stay at home. Once these tasks were done, she had leisure to sit down and think about the trip to Las Palmas. Rauwerd hadn't told her when it would be but she would need clothes. She found paper and pen and made a list, a pleasant occupation which kept her occupied until lunchtime.

She had an unexpected visit from Rauwerd's mother in the afternoon. 'I should have telephoned you, my dear,' said that lady, 'but I had a sudden impulse to come and see you and have a chat. We so enjoyed ourselves the other evening and I am so glad that you have Rose Werdmer ter Sane for a friend. She is a dear girl.' She settled herself comfortably and said that yes, she would indeed stay for tea. 'Rauwerd will be home?' she asked.

'No, he is in Brussels. But he will be back later on this evening.'

'He's a busy man, what with his practice and the hospital beds he has. And now this lecturing. You feel lonely, Matilda?'

'Well, no. You see, everything is strange to me; I go shopping with Bep and take Dickens for a walk when he hasn't gone with Rauwerd; and I like doing the flowers—and in a house as large as this one, that takes some time. I am now to start Dutch lessons, too . . .'

She poured the tea and they sipped it in pleasant friendliness. 'We had Professor Vouters to dinner yesterday—I liked him—and a friend of Rauwerd's, Nikky van Wijk.'

Mevrouw van Kempler bit into a wafer-thin biscuit. 'Ah, yes, a striking-looking woman, I always think.'

'Oh, very, and so beautifully dressed. I've always envied that kind of silvery fair hair.'

'Out of a bottle,' said Mevrouw van Kempler, surprisingly.

Matilda stifled a giggle and then said soberly, 'I mean to like her because she is such an old friend of Rauwerd's. I think she's very clever and that is nice for him. I mean, he is clever, too, isn't he?'

'Oh, very,' agreed his mother, 'but not with everything, my dear.'

There didn't seem to be anything to say to that. Matilda said chattily, 'He is going to Las Palmas and I'm to go with him. I've never been there; it will be lovely . . .'

'Ah, yes. When do you go?'

'I don't know; he forgot to say.' She added hastily, 'He's so very busy.'

Mevrouw van Kempler said, 'H'm,' and then, 'I must be going, my dear.'

Matilda accompanied her outside to the street where she had parked a rather elderly Rover. She kissed Matilda briefly before she got into the car and drove away a great deal too fast.

Matilda was about to sit down to her solitary dinner that evening when Rose telephoned them to invite them to dinner on the following Saturday. 'Just the four of us,' she explained, 'so that you can get to know us a bit better. Eight o'clock—we'll expect you unless something crops up.'

Rauwerd got home just before ten o'clock. He looked tired and she hurried to get the coffee and sandwiches Bep had left ready in the kitchen. He was surprised when she came into the room with the tray. 'Where is Bep? Or Jan?'

'I told them to go to bed—they have a long day, you know. I was wondering what there would be for Emma to do when she comes, but she's just what is needed—another pair of hands.'

She poured his coffee and handed him the plate of sandwiches.

'Should we have some more staff? Aren't there two maids who come in each day?'

'Yes, but they go at six o'clock and they don't come at all on Sundays. That is where Emma is going to fill a gap. They'll be glad of some help and she'll be so pleased to have a job.' She went and sat down opposite him. 'Did you have a successful day?'

He nodded. And that was to be all, she realised.

'Rose has asked us to dinner next Saturday—just us and them. She said to let her know if you couldn't make it.'

'I should be free. I try to keep the weekends open, though I don't always succeed. Do you want to do anything tomorrow other than fetching Emma?'

'No, thank you.'

'Then we'll go to morning church and have a lazy day until we leave for Schiphol. I forgot to tell you that I've asked your teacher to come for drinks before lunch tomorrow—you can get to know each other. He'd like to start this week, if that's all right with you.'

'I'll be glad to start.' She poured more coffee. 'Rauwerd, this trip to Las Palmas, when will it be?'

'Two weeks' time. You'll need clothes. We shall fly over and stay until the seminar is over, then have a week off.'

'I shall enjoy that. Will it be warm there?'

'Pleasantly so, I hope. But take something warm to wear if we go into the mountains.'

He sounded faintly bored, and she made haste to change the conversation. 'Your mother came to tea. It was very pleasant.'

'I'm glad.'

He didn't want to talk any more. She said goodnight quietly and went up to bed, stifling her hurt because he didn't need her company.

They breakfasted together, exchanging platitudes, and presently walked along the canal to church. Even though she couldn't understand a word of it, Matilda found it comforting, and some of the hymn tunes were familiar. After the service there were various friends and acquaintances of Rauwerd's to meet. They went back to give her teacher a drink and then to lunch and have a quiet hour or so sitting in the drawing-room. There were no Sunday papers in Holland, but there were books and magazines in plenty. They sat there, she quiet as a mouse, reading a book she had no interest in because Rauwerd was immersed in a sheaf of papers and quite obviously didn't want to be disturbed.

Schiphol was barely half an hour's drive away. They had tea a little earlier than usual and got into the car. Rauwerd had little to say, which made it difficult for Matilda to voice something she felt had to be said.

'It's very kind of you to have Emma,' she began. 'I'm very grateful and I know that she is, too.'

'My dear girl, you said yourself that she will fill a gap in the household. I am the one to be grateful and I'm sure that Jan and Bep will be.'

'Oh, I do hope they'll like each other.'

She need not have worried. Emma, still nervous from the flight, so happy to see Matilda again, became, in some miraculous way, a member of the household the moment she set foot inside the front door. She was borne away by Bep to have her tea and then followed Matilda upstairs to her room.

'Why, Miss Tilly, it's luxury! Look at that chair and the TV and a bathroom all to myself.' A few difficult tears trickled down her cheeks. 'I never thought it'd end like this—you so 'appy and this lovely 'ouse and me in the lap of luxury. I only 'opes I'll earn me keep.'

Matilda flung a comforting arm about her shoulders. 'Of course you will, Emma. Bep and Jan need you; there is so much you can do to help and they are both elderly, you know. It means that they can take things a little more easily. There are two daily maids so there is no hard work but there's masses of silver and glass and furniture to be polished. You're just what is needed.'

She left Emma to unpack and went to tidy herself for dinner. When she went downstairs Rauwerd was on the phone in the hall. She hurried past him, unwilling to eavesdrop, but she couldn't help hearing him say with clear deliberation, 'No, Nikky, I can't manage this evening and I'm pretty busy during the week. Get your *notaris* to deal with it and let me know if you have any difficulties.'

He followed Matilda into the drawing-room. 'Nikky

is the most unbusinesslike woman I have ever met.' He went to pour the drinks. 'But I've no intention of puzzling over stocks and shares this evening. I prefer to be by my own fireside.'

He turned to look at her and she switched the peevish frown on her face to an expression of casual interest. She hoped that she had done it smartly enough. 'I should think that stocks and shares are very complicated things; I wouldn't know one from the other.'

'No, perhaps not, Tilly, but I fancy you would make it your business to find out. You're self-reliant, or do I mean self-sufficient?'

'Neither of them sound like me.' And because he was staring at her so hard she plunged into talk. 'Emma is so happy. She's not at all worried about being in another country; I dare say she'll pick up more Dutch in a week than I shall in six months.'

Rauwerd laughed. 'Not if old Professor Tacx has anything to do with it. What did you think of him? We must have him to dinner one evening.'

'I liked him, though he seemed a bit fierce.'

'Just his manner. He'll make you work hard.'

'Well, the sooner I can speak and understand Dutch the better. I shall do my best.'

They dined unhurriedly, carrying on a desultory conversation which for some reason Matilda found reassuring, perhaps because it made her feel so secure and married. But her new-found content received a jolt as they sat over their coffee.

'I have been waiting for you to ask about Nikky.' Rauwerd's voice was bland and faintly amused.

Matilda took a big sip of coffee and scalded her tongue. 'Why?' she asked baldly. 'You told me that she was an old friend. I have no intention of prying.' She went on matter-of-factly, 'It isn't as if I were in—in love with you and wanted to know everything about you.' And, when he didn't say anything, 'I'm quite content. That sounds selfish, but I don't mean it to be. What I'm trying to say is that you have no need to worry about me. I don't expect you to change your life just because you married me . . .'

He raised his eyebrows. 'No? Should I feel flattered, I wonder, or downcast at the idea of making so little impression upon you?'

She blushed. 'You know I don't mean that. You said before you married me that we would get on well together—that's what you want, isn't it?'

He said slowly. 'Yes. That's what I wanted, Matilda.' He got up from his chair. 'I've some telephoning to do. Why don't you arrange to meet Rose and do your shopping together? I'll have to be in Amsterdam tomorrow, you can drive there with me and I'll pick you up on my way home.'

'That sounds a marvellous idea. I'll telephone her in the morning.' She picked up the knitting lying on the table beside her. 'I'll go and make sure that Emma is all right. I dare say she'd like a gossip; she must be feeling a bit strange. Then I'll go to bed, so I'll say goodnight.'

She gave him a friendly nod and smile; if he didn't want her company then she would be the last person to let him know that she minded.

Emma was in her room, arranging her bits and pieces just so. Far from feeling strange she appeared to have settled in without a qualm; she liked Jan and Bep and, with Jan's translating, had already agreed to take over several chores from Bep. 'Ever so 'appy, I am, love,' she told Matilda. 'I reckon we're two lucky ones, you with that lovely man for a 'usband and me falling on me feet, and all thanks to 'im.'

Matilda agreed with her, wished her goodnight and went to her own bed. She had, she reminded herself, a great deal to be thankful for. She lay awake a long time, planning her clothes for the forthcoming trip. But her last thought was of Rauwerd.

Rose was delighted to go shopping. She took Matilda to Maison de Bonneterie and the two of them spent a delightful hour or so choosing an outfit suitable for Las Palmas in the spring. Having money to spend made it much easier, of course, but Matilda refused to be carried away by the more exotic garments on display and settled for a cotton jersey dress and matching long coat, several cotton dresses in bright colours, and two crêpe evening dresses which would take up no room in her luggage and wouldn't crush either. She did allow herself to be extravagant over swimsuits and their accompanying cover-ups; surely while Rauwerd was at his seminar she would be able to spend hours on a beach somewhere or, failing that, in the hotel swimming-pool.

The two of them took a taxi back to Rose's home, a lovely old house in a narrow street tucked away from the city centre. They had lunch, played with little Sybren, examined Matilda's purchases and gossiped until Sybren arrived at the same time as the tea-tray was brought in and, hard on his heels, Rauwerd.

Rose had flown into Sybren's arms the moment he arrived and Matilda hoped that the casual, 'Hello, Tilly' would pass unnoticed when Rauwerd joined them. He made things easier by leaning down and

kissing her cheek—a gesture without warmth, and not
to be compared with Sybren's fierce hug for his small
wife, but at least it was something.

They spent an hour—a happy one—before leaving,
with the promise that they would return on Saturday
for dinner.

'Finished your shopping?' Rauwerd wanted to know
as he drove back.

'Yes, thank you. I don't need to take many clothes,
do I? You'll be busy for the first week, won't you?'

'Only until seven or thereabouts in the evening. I
shall need to relax then—dinner, dancing.' He added
airily, 'And I thought we might hire a car and see
something of the island.'

At least two more evening dresses, she reflected, and
perhaps more cotton tops and skirts. She said, speaking
her thoughts out loud, 'I'm not very happy in slacks.'

His firm mouth curved into a smile. 'Then skirts, my
dear, although I should have thought that slacks were
invented for legs like yours.'

A compliment. The first he had ever paid her. She
would go to that chic little boutique in Leiden and
invest in a couple of pairs—pastel colours; they would
go well with the floral tops she had already bought.

She said quietly, 'Thank you. Have you been there?'

'A couple of times. I think you will like it.'

She bought the slacks the next day and then went for
her first Dutch lesson. Professor Tacx was a dear old
thing although she quickly discovered that he was
going to be a hard taskmaster. Her brain addled with
Dutch verbs, she went back home with enough work to
keep her busy for the rest of the week, only she would
have to get it done before then for she was to have

another lesson on Friday.

At dinner that evening Rauwerd asked, 'Lesson go well?'

'Oh, yes, I enjoyed it. How long will it take before I can speak Dutch?'

'Some months, but you'll be able to understand it before then and make yourself understood. Shopping and so forth. I must remember to speak Dutch to you and, of course, you can practise on Bep and Jan.'

'Should Emma have lessons?'

'She'll pick up all she needs just being with Bep and Jan. Lessons would only bother her. Our grammar is quite different and I doubt if she will want to read Dutch; there are plenty of paperbacks and papers in English. Tell me what she enjoys reading and I'll arrange for it to be sent.'

'That's kind of you. She seems quite at home already.'

'Good. And you, Matilda? Do you feel at home?'

She raised serious eyes to him. 'Yes, Rauwerd. I love this house and I like your parents very much. I only hope that I'll be a help to you—giving dinner parties and entertaining your friends.'

'Ah, yes. When we get back we must give a small party, don't you think? And there will be the Spring Ball at the medical school and several evening functions to attend, here and in den Haag.'

'I had a note from Beatrix Thenus asking me to go to coffee on Thursday. She wants to talk to me about joining a fund-raising scheme—something to do with children ...'

He glanced across the table at her. 'Yes? I imagine you will be asked to attend similar functions as well as innumerable charitable organisations.'

'You would like me to join them?'

'My dear, you must do as you please. They are mostly worthwhile and I can't imagine that you will want to fritter away your days. I'm involved in several schemes to do with children; it would be nice if you shared my interest.'

'I'd like that.' She was eager to hear more but his laconic, 'Good. Shall we have coffee in the drawing room?' stopped her from asking any more questions.

The week came to its end with another lesson from Professor Tacx and a delightful dinner with Rose and Sybren. The next week went as smoothly, with more lessons, packing for their trip and an almost imperceptible taking over of the household reins. She was careful not to trespass on Bep's domain in the kitchen and the house, but she began to deal with bills and accounts, spent time with Bep learning the price of things and what to buy, and she went to the cellars with Jan and inspected their contents under his knowledgable eye. She wasn't likely to be called upon to choose wine, but she was abysmally ignorant on such matters.

Any qualms she might have had about Emma settling down were quickly put at rest; Emma declared herself to be completely at home and content. There were tasks enough in the old house; beautiful furniture to polish, the linen cupboards to keep tidy, smalls to wash, clothes to press. She had never been so happy, she assured Matilda. Ignorance of the language didn't bother her in the least; she trotted off to the shops with Bep, and in her free time took herself off to the town to explore on her own. She and Bep also shared an enthusiasm for knitting and she was already busy on a

pullover for Rauwerd, a thank you present for his
kindness.

Matilda had searched the bookshops for information
about Las Palmas, and by the time they were due to
leave she had worked her way through several
guidebooks and a brochure or two, so that she wasn't
completely ignorant about the city and the island. She
wore the coat and dress in which to travel and was
conscious of Rauwerd's approval as they got into the
car.

They drove to Schiphol not saying much, with Jan
sitting in the back so that he might drive the car back to
Leiden, and once at the airport they went aboard
immediately. How quickly one got used to comfort and
ease, reflected Matilda, settling into her first-class seat.
It was a mid-morning flight and the plane was only half
full. She looked from the porthole as they took off and
then, since Rauwerd had opened his briefcase and
taken out a sheaf of papers, buried her pretty nose in
one of the magazines he had bought her.

When their lunch was served he put his work away.
'The nice part about you, Matilda,' he observed, 'is
that I don't have to worry about ruffling your feelings
if I need to do some work. You like flying?'

Her feelings, if he did not know it, were ruffled, but
she said matter-of-factly, 'I'm not sure. Uncle and I,
when we went on holiday, which wasn't often, used to
take the car and tour around Britain.'

He looked surprised. 'This is your first flight? My
dear girl, if I had known I wouldn't have occupied
myself with these notes.'

He sounded concerned and she said quickly, 'Oh,
that's all right, I'm not nervous.'

He talked as they ate lunch and she felt relaxed and soothed. He could be a delightful companion when he wanted to be, and very amusing, too.

'We are staying at a rather nice hotel, not very near the shops or the beach, but there is a car waiting for us. It's called the Santa Catalina and, since I'd rather you didn't go out on your own, it won't matter that it's a little way out of the centre of the city.'

She received this high-handed arrangement of her days silently and he went on, 'I'll be at the conference and various meetings each morning, back at the hotel for lunch and then back at three o'clock until about seven in the evening. Everything closes in the afternoons but we can swim or drive around the island. There is plenty of night-life . . .'

'Clubs and things?' asked Matilda doubtfully.

He smiled. 'They abound. I dare say we shall be content with a visit to one of the bars on Las Canteras beach and perhaps some dancing. The hotel is very comfortable but quiet, but there is nothing to stop us driving to Maspalomas—Sybren was telling me of a good hotel there where we can dance or visit the casino.'

Perhaps not high-handed after all. 'That sounds fun,' she said.

'For our second week I thought we might go to Tenerife. I've booked at the Botanico in Puerto de la Cruz; there's a dance floor and cabaret and it's in a small park. I think you'll like it. We'll have a car there, too, and explore.'

It all sounded marvellous; by the time the plane landed Matilda was happy and excited.

The car was waiting at the airport and Rauwerd

drove the fourteen miles into the city and on to their hotel. Matilda was instantly impressed; it was built in the Spanish style and lay well away from the road, surrounded by trees and a rather pretty garden. Once inside she could see that it was pleasantly and comfortably furnished. Their rooms were on the first floor and were large and airy and overlooked a small park. Altogether charming, she decided, and told Rauwerd so when he came into her room.

'I've asked for some tea to be sent up,' he told her, 'and when you've unpacked we might go for a short run in the car so that you can get your bearings. Unless you are tired.'

'Tired! It would be criminal to be tired—just look at those trees . . .' She craned her neck over the balcony. 'And geraniums, hundreds of them.'

After tea they drove through the busy city and along the coast road to Arucas, a charming little town of white-walled houses, dominated by a modern cathedral. They returned along a winding road which brought them back to Las Palmas, humming with evening traffic, had a drink in the bar and then went to change for dinner.

A delightful evening, decided Matilda, laying her sleepy head on the pillow later that night.

The evenings which followed it were just as delightful. True, she found the days lonely; there was a limit to the amount of sunbathing and swimming in the hotel pool she could enjoy. By the time Rauwerd returned in the evening, she was more than glad to see him, for lunch, although they ate it together, was usually a hurried meal, for, contrary to custom, the members at the conference had decided to do without a

siesta. But even though she was tempted, she stayed at
the hotel and was rewarded for this by evenings spent
driving to Maspalomas to dance or to stroll along the
esplanade to one of the numerous bars, or to try their
luck at the casino.

On the last day, after Rauwerd had got back from his
final conference, he took her into the city and wandered
around the shops, waiting patiently while she bought
embroidery, leather handbags for Emma and Bep, and
exquisitely stitched handkerchiefs for the maids, and
when she admired a beautifully made silver bracelet, he
bought it for her and clasped it around her wrist.

She thanked him a little shyly. 'It's been a lovely
week,' she told him and he nodded.

'Next week will be even better', he observed.

They went by hydrofoil to Tenerife, transferred to
the car waiting at the quay, and drove to the hotel.
Puerto de la Cruz captured Matilda's fancy at once and
the hotel, a short distance from the centre of the town,
appeared delightful. It was surrounded by a large
garden with banana plantations beyond it, and was
close to the botanical gardens. Inside it was as superbly
comfortable as one could wish for. She was surprised to
find that they had a suite, their rooms opening on to a
sitting-room whose doors gave on to a patio and a
swimming pool.

'Just for us?' Matilda wanted to know.

'Yes.' He was watching her happy face. 'You like it?'

'It's super. What did you say was the name of this
hotel?'

'Botanico—it's close to the botanical gardens.'

'Is the pool heated?'

'Yes. Shall we have a swim before dinner?'

She wasn't a good swimmer but she felt safe enough, for the pool wasn't large and, besides, Rauwerd was there. She left him still ploughing strongly through the clear water and went to dress. The patterned chiffon, she decided, and debated whether she should buy another evening gown; the guests in the bigger hotels dressed for the evening and she had only the two crêpe dresses besides.

The chiffon did her justice; she did her face carefully, brushed her hair until it shone and went into the sitting-room. Rauwerd was already there. 'Shall I ring for drinks or shall we go down to the bar?' he asked.

She felt suddenly shy of him. 'Oh, the bar.' She spoke too quickly and he gave her a hard stare before opening the door. She caught the tail end of it and wondered if he was annoyed, but the smile which followed the stare was bland, so she decided that she had been mistaken.

The evening was delightful; they dined and danced and presently wished each other goodnight. If every day was going to be like this one, Matilda told herself, then the week was going to be a success; she had felt at ease with him as well as so much enjoying his company. She got into bed, eager for the morning so that she would be with him again.

They had agreed to swim before breakfast and he was already in the pool when she lowered herself cautiously into the shallow end. But once in, she found the water exactly right and the morning sun, shining from a blue sky, was warm on her as she swam sedately backwards and forwards.

'Why not try something else?' asked Rauwerd,

loitering along beside her. 'The crawl, perhaps? I'll stay beside you.'

She splashed and splattered her way to and fro and finally she gave up. 'I don't think I'm built for it,' she observed, 'and I hate to get underwater.'

His eyes flickered over her shapely person. 'Perhaps not,' he agreed gravely while his eyes gleamed beneath their lids. 'Shall we have breakfast on the balcony? I'll order it while you are dressing. Orange juice and croissants and coffee?'

They spent the day pottering round the shops and having another swim at the lido on the promenade before lunching out of doors at a nearby restaurant. In the afternoon they went back to the shops along the seafront because Matilda had seen a dress she had rather liked in the window of one of the chic boutiques there.

'Buy it,' said Rauwerd lazily, 'I like you in pink.'

The dress, very pale pink voile with a tiny bodice and yards of stole to match it, was a perfect fit. At the elegant jeweller's shop next door Rauwerd bought her pink coral earrings to go with it.

Another lovely day, mused Matilda, sliding into bed hours later. The dress had been a success and they had danced for hours. She sighed with a half-understood happiness and went instantly to sleep.

They would take the car in the afternoon, said Rauwerd over breakfast the next morning, and go north through the mountains to Bajamar. 'It's a small seaside resort, not particularly pretty, but to get to it one must drive along a magnificent road with some splendid views. We'll stop at the Pico del Inglés and you will be able to see for yourself.'

They went to the lido again after breakfast and had an early lunch at the hotel. It was still a bright day but as they drove north they could see dark clouds above the mountains ahead of them.

'I'll take you to the African market tomorrow morning,' said Rauwerd. 'This place we're coming to is San Andrés—a fishing village.'

They didn't go right into the village but turned sharply and began to climb, presently leaving the scattering of houses behind them. The road was rather frightening, cut into the sides of the mountains looming all around them with a steep gorge on one side of it and towering sombre rock on the other. It wound up and up in a continuous bend and from time to time made a U-turn so tight that the car seemed to hang over the edge of the road as Rauwerd pulled it round. The higher they drove, the more awesome were their surroundings, with clouds dipping and swirling through the giant pines and beech trees, cutting them off from the outside world.

'You're not enjoying it?' said Rauwerd presently.

'Oh, yes, it's magnificent ... Well, perhaps not quite. How did you know?'

'Your hands, so tightly clasped; besides, I can feel you stiffen at every bend.'

She said quickly, anxious to reassure him, 'It's really an experience—I wouldn't have missed it for the world.'

He gave a short laugh. 'All the same, you're scared. I'm sorry.'

'No, no, not that. You're here.' She spoke simply. 'With anyone else I would be, though. I'm overawed; it's so lonely, it could be the end of the world.' And, to make sure that he didn't think that she was complaining, 'It's a marvellous road . . .'

'Yes. Well used, too, though there is not much on it today.'

He took another U-turn and she remembered not to clasp her hands, only to grip them hard and let out a startled breath as he braked hard at the end of an S-bend to avoid two cars ahead of them, tangled together on the road. They must have met head on, for the back wheels of one of them were hanging over the edge of the ravine and the bonnet of the second car was crushed against the rock of the mountain side.

Rauwerd slid to a halt. His calm, 'Dear me,' soothed Matilda into instant obedience when he said, 'Take that red scarf of yours, my dear, and go back to the bend and hang it on to a handy branch—anything, just as long as it can be seen.'

He turned to study the road ahead of them. The road wound round the mountain in a wide sweep; any car coming that way would be able to see them.

'Off you go and take care.' He leaned across to open her door and kissed her hard. 'I'm going to have a look.'

Matilda got out of the car aware, over and above the horrors of the moment, of his kiss. She found a branch, tied the scarf—a new one she had bought only that morning—and hurried back, to stop short at the sight of Rauwerd, head and shoulders through the window of the car teetering so dangerously on the edge of the road.

'Don't come any nearer, Tilly.' His voice sounded loud and calm and she did as she was told, watching him with her heart in her mouth as he took the wheel and slowly pushed the car away from the edge. He emerged then, dusting his hands, breathing rather hard.

'We must get that man out—thank heaven you're a big strong girl.' He ignored her indignant glance. 'He is unconscious. There are two in the other car, but I think he is the more urgent.'

He had the door open and was heaving gently at the man behind the wheel. Matilda didn't wait to be told what to do; she could see for herself. They laid him gently on the side of the road and she fetched a rug from their car and put it under his head.

'The others first,' said Rauwerd and wrenched the second car's door open. The woman in the back was easily lifted clear but the driver took a good deal longer. He looked in a bad way, his breathing shallow and his colour ashen.

'Undo his shirt,' said Rauwerd and, 'Just as I thought, his lung is pierced—look at that bruise. See what you can do about it, Tilly.'

Just as though I had a dressing trolley handy, thought Matilda, and ripped off the hem of the flowered cotton skirt she was wearing. It was first aid of the crudest kind but at least it stopped the bleeding and his pulse when she took it was regular, even if it was weak.

She crossed the road to where Rauwerd was bending over the woman. 'Broken arm, concussion, a nasty cut from glass.'

She tore another strip from her skirt and used it to good effect.

'I need a sling,' said Rauwerd.

There was a Gucci scarf still in its elegant packet; she had bought it for Rose. She went to the car and fetched it and offered it silently.

'I'll buy you a dozen,' said Rauwerd.

The second man was a more serious matter; his chest was already showing massive bruising, he was cold and clammy and his pulse was a mere thread. Over and above that he had a broken leg. Rauwerd straightened it as best he could and tied it to the sound one with the man's leather belt while Tilly found cushions and more rugs.

Rauwerd got to his feet. 'I'm going to drive back until I find a phone—there was a house a few miles back. It'll be light for some hours yet and I'll leave you the torch.'

'You're going to leave me here?' Indignation and fright made her voice squeaky.

'I must, Tilly, dear. I can't let you drive, you couldn't on this road.'

She swallowed panic. 'You won't be long?'

'Not a second longer than I must be. If anyone comes along, stop them and make them stay, too.'

'Make them stay—how?'

He grinned. 'You are a beautiful girl—they'll stay.' He bent and kissed her cheek. 'Take care,' he told her and got into the car, reversed carefully round the bend and, after what seemed an age, turned it. Moments later she saw the car going dangerously fast along the road curving round the next ravine.

There wasn't much she could do but she did it faithfully—pulses and breathing to check and colour to watch. After an hour she sighed with relief to find them all still alive.

It was another half-hour before she was able to see the car intermittently as it climbed the steep curving road below her, then a further ten minutes before Rauwerd pulled up gently beside her and got out.

The wish to fling herself at him and burst into tears was overwhelming but she fought it hard.

'That's my girl. How are they? There is a police car and an ambulance on their way from Bandama—there's a first-aid clinic there and they can be sent on to Santa Cruz as soon as they have been examined.' He patted her shoulders and went to look at the three prone figures.

The police were there five minutes later; she heard the siren long before she saw the blue light flashing along the road ahead of them. They didn't waste much time in talk but set to, with Rauwerd helping them to move the wrecked cars to the side of the road. They had just finished when the ambulance arrived.

It took time to load the three patients into it; first it had to turn round, for it would have to return the way it had come from Bandama. When it was at last on its way, there were questions to be answered for the police, taking twice as long because every word had to be translated by Rauwerd. But they finished at last, shook hands all round, and, in their turn, drove back the way they had come.

It was quiet once more and the mist had turned the afternoon into twilight evening. Rauwerd walked back to the bend and fetched her scarf and then stood holding it, smiling at her. She had a nice safe feeling seeing him standing there. It was strange to think that when they had first met she had thought she disliked him. She stared back at him, her lovely mouth slightly open with the sudden surprise of knowing that she was in love with him.

CHAPTER SEVEN

MATILDA felt like someone who had taken a step which wasn't there at the bottom of a staircase. With difficulty she closed her mouth but she couldn't stop the colour leaving her cheeks; emotion had washed over her leaving her with her bones changed to water, and she almost choked with her efforts not to voice her feelings.

Rauwerd was watching her closely, no longer smiling. 'Are you all right?' he wanted to know. 'Come and sit in the car.' He came and took her arm and the touch of his hand started her shaking. 'We'll drive on to Bajamar and find you a stiff drink. You were marvellous, Tilly.' He glanced down at her ruined skirt, smiling a little.

'Well, I am a nurse,' she mumbled. 'It's only that it was so sudden. I'm quite all right now.'

She was still trembling, but not because of the accident. This nonsense must stop! she told herself silently as he started the car and drove on once more.

The road was just as bad but it could be no worse than the last hour or two; she averted her eyes from the ravines below and after a few miles heaved a sigh of relief as trees closed in on them on either side and the cloud blotted out the awe-inspiring views.

They began to go downhill and presently the road wound itself gently down to green fields and rows of tomatoes and potatoes and wild flowers rioting at the roadside. She could see the sea now and a cluster of white-walled and red-roofed houses—Bajamar, a disappointingly ordinary little town with one or two hotels, a row of shops facing the sea, and a series of pools corralled from the ocean. Rauwerd stopped before the row of shops, all of them still open, and ushered Matilda into a coffee shop at the end of the row. It was pleasant inside, full of customers, but there was an empty table in a corner. He sat her down at it and ordered tea for her and coffee for himself. He ordered two brandies, too, and made her drink hers at once. That, and the hot, milkless tea, stopped her trembling and sent the colour back into her cheeks. She had had time, during the drive down the mountains, to pull herself together.

Rauwerd ordered more tea for her. 'That's better. It was quite an experience, wasn't it?'

Common sense had taken over once more. She said steadily, 'Yes, I shall never forget it.' She wasn't thinking of the accident.

They sat for half an hour, during which time Rauwerd carried on a placid flow of small talk, and presently she was able to get into the car beside him, carefully not looking at him, although it was difficult for her to keep her eyes off his large, capable hands on the wheel.

He drove back another way. They had driven through Santa Cruz on their way to the mountains; now he followed the coast south for a few miles before joining the main road at Tacoronte and so along the coast still to Puerto de la Cruz. Back at the hotel he recommended that she should take a bath and, if she felt like it, a nap before changing for dinner and she complied, grateful for the chance to have time to herself in which to think.

She lay in tepid, fragrant water and tried to see into the future. Ten minutes' hard thinking convinced her that this wasn't at all a wise thing to do. It was going to be a difficult enough task living with Rauwerd on the friendly casual basis he took for granted, taking no part in his life other than running his household and playing hostess to his friends. Which brought her to another worry: Nikky. She hadn't liked her in the first place; now she seethed at the mere thought of her. She would have to form a plan of campaign if she intended to be happy ever after, and that meant Rauwerd falling in love with her ...

He had shown no romantic interest in her so far; pleasure in her company perhaps, but no more than that. She would have to change, become more like Nikky—lose weight for a start; Nikky had almost no curves. Matilda studied her own charming person with a frowning eye. And a new hairstyle. There was a beauty salon in Leiden; she would go there and have a facial and make-up. She would have to diet and perhaps have sessions of those slimming techniques she had never thought much of. She couldn't do much about it until they got back to Leiden, only eat less ...

She wore the pink with the stole again, ate a splendid dinner, quite forgetful of her resolve to slim drastically, and danced until one o'clock in the morning. Rauwerd was his usual calm self, although a little withdrawn, which was just as well for it reminded her that from his point of view, at least, nothing had changed. Even if her whole world had been turned upside down, she must never let him see it.

He took her to the African market after breakfast the next morning; they strolled from stall to stall, looking at the cheeses and fruit and the fish and flowers, and then they went to the lido and swam and sat in the sun with fruit drinks. They were both nicely tanned; Matilda was beginning to look like a magnificent gypsy and Rauwerd's hair had become pale gilt.

They sat for an hour doing nothing after lunch, in the cool of their sitting-room, and then, after an early cup of tea, he drove her to Icod de los Vinos to see the Dragon Tree. 'It's reputed to be three thousand years old,' he told her, 'and it certainly looks it.'

They got out of the car and sat in its shade until a busload of tourists sent them on their way again. They were much nearer Pico del Tiede now but Rauwerd turned away from it. Instead he drove back the way they had come and turned off to La Orotava, where he parked the car and took her wandering up and down its steep streets to admire the lovely old houses and pleasing buildings and presently to sit outside in Calle San Francisco, the most interesting street of them all, and to drink small cups of dark, rich coffee in a café. Later they went back to their hotel, driving through the lovely Orotava Valley, bright with flowers and every kind of tree and bush. The road was a series of S-bends, but the scenery wasn't sombre or frightening and Matilda loved every moment of it.

She told Rauwerd so when they got back to the hotel, lifting a happy face to his, carefree of anything but the delight of the moment. 'Oh, it was gorgeous,' she told him. 'What shall we do tomorrow?'

He smiled down at her and then bent and kissed her cheek. 'I'm glad you enjoyed it, my dear. Supposing we drive right round the island? We can take our swimming things and stop somewhere quiet for lunch.'

They danced again after dinner. Such a pity, grieved Matilda silently, that when they got back to Leiden she would spend her evenings endlessly alone or entertaining his friends—Nikky ... She shuddered at the very thought of her and his arm tightened round her. 'You're cold? You feel all right?'

She assured him that she had never felt better, speaking into the crisp whiteness of his shirt front, afraid to meet his eyes.

It was remarkable, she reflected as she got ready for bed, how well she had taken herself in hand. No one would ever guess that she was besotted over her husband, least of all her husband. She derived a wry satisfaction from the thoughts and then burst into tears.

The drive round the island took almost all day, for they loitered to admire the views, wander round the cathedral at La Laguna, and drink coffee in a pavement café before following the road down the east coast, stopping again at Candelaria so that Matilda might marvel at the black sand and the statues of Guanches lining the sea front. The country began to change, its vivid greenness giving way to dry earth, although the coastline was enchanting. They didn't stop at El Medano—obviously it was a budding tourist centre—but went on to the Costa del Silencia, with its rocky

coast and peace and quiet. They had lunch at the
charming little hotel there, then found a small cove,
nicely sheltered from the sun, and presently they swam.

When they drove on later they didn't stop at Los
Cristianos but paused to drink their tea in Los Gigantes
before making their way back to the hotel. A lovely day
rounded off with a delightful evening.

The last day came too soon and they decided to go to
the lido once more and do nothing but lie in the sun and
swim. They had explored the island thoroughly and
wandered round the shops and now next day they
would fly back to Holland and she would be lucky if she
saw Rauwerd for more than an hour or so each day.
They wandered down to the pool and found long
chairs, and Matilda, in a vivid bikini, veiled by a thin
matching wrap, her dark hair crowned by a large straw
hat, was unaware of the stares of the men around her.

Rauwerd settled himself beside her, chuckling. 'I'm
not surprised that you are collecting leers from all sides,
Tilly—you look good enough to eat, which is more
than I can say for those around us. I've never seen so
much bare flesh so unwisely exposed, and I'm not
speaking as a medical man.' He turned over on his back
and looked sideways at her.

'Have I ever told you that you're a beautiful young
woman?'

She was glad of the wide brim of her sunhat; it
screened her face nicely from his stare. She said quietly,
'No, you haven't and I'm not—it's just the blue sky
and the sun and a very expensive beach outfit . . .' She
went on slowly, 'I'm the same girl as I always was, only
dressed differently.'

'Not quite the same girl,' he reminded her. 'You're married now.' He spoke silkily and she bit back the retort which sprung to her lips. It would never do to destroy the still shaky foundations of a deeper friendship between them. She rolled over and smiled widely at him.

'I like being married and I've loved our holiday. I hope we'll be able to do it again some time!'

He said lazily, 'I'm a busy man, but we'll see what we can do.'

'Have you enjoyed it, too?'

His eyes were half shut. 'Oh, indeed, yes.' And then, 'Shall we swim?'

It was raining at Schiphol when, well on schedule, they landed, and Holland looked flat and uninteresting after the mountains of the Canary Islands, but once in Leiden Matilda forgot all that. Jan had met them at the airport with a wide smile, but that was nothing compared with the warmth of their welcome home: Bep and Emma waiting on the doorstep and the two daily maids hovering in the background. Matilda tidied herself and hurried downstairs to join Rauwerd in the drawing-room, to find the tea tray already there and him immersed in a great pile of letters.

She poured the tea and he accepted his cup with a vague nod, so that she went to sit opposite him, as still as a mouse, sipping from her own cup. It was with a sinking heart that she realised that he had become immediately immersed in his correspondence. She drank a second cup of tea and, since he seemed unaware of her, went upstairs to her room and unpacked her

things, while Emma fussed gently around, collecting
things for cleaning and the laundry. That didn't take
long; Emma went away presently and Matilda sat
down before her dressing-table, did her face and her
hair and then changed into a pretty dress. It was almost
time for dinner; surely Rauwerd would have finished
his post by now. She was half way down the staircase
when she heard his voice; she couldn't understand
what he was saying but she heard him exclaim 'Nikky'
in a laughing voice and then '*Tot straks*', and that
meant, near enough, presently.

She went on down the stairs and her heart went
down into her pretty slippers as she went; Nikky had
seemed far away and forgotten while they had been on
holiday, but of course that wasn't the case; she had
been there all the time, ready to pounce the moment
they got back to Leiden. She went into the dining-
room, outwardly serene, inwardly seething.

Rauwerd was standing by the window, looking into
the street. 'Ah, there you are, my dear. Will you forgive
me if I leave you to dine alone? Something has come up
which needs dealing with at once.'

'The hospital?' asked Matilda mildly.

'Nikky. She has become so used to me helping her
when she gets into difficulties about something; I can't
let her down.' He poured their drinks and handed her a
glass of sherry. 'Nice to be home, isn't it?'

'Delightful,' said Matilda evenly. 'Don't let me keep
you if you want to leave right away. I'll just go to the
kitchen and tell Bep to do something about dinner.' She
flashed him a brilliant smile, put down her untouched
sherry and left him there.

Bep was puzzled and put out. She had planned a splendid meal for their homecoming and when Matilda told her that the doctor wouldn't be there to eat it, she almost burst into tears.

'But I shall enjoy it,' declared Matilda stoutly, 'and I'm famished. Perhaps you would leave sandwiches for the doctor? I don't know when he will be back; very late I expect.'

She was crossing the hall as he opened the front door. 'Have a nice evening,' she said flippantly. 'It'll make a welcome change for you.' She swept into the drawing-room and shut the door on his surprised face.

Matilda had plenty of time to think the situation over. She had dined in solitary state, eating something of everything so as not to upset Bep and then, after a suitable interval, going up to her room. But not to sleep. She settled into one of the comfortable chairs and, clearing her head of rage, envy and near panic, made plans for a future which, at the moment, didn't look too rosy. Obviously she had been living in cloud cuckoo land, so she must forget the two weeks that they had just spent together. Rauwerd had wanted a wife to run his house, and come home to, someone who would cope with the social side of his life without bothering him so that he could get on with his work. And Nikky, said a small voice, interrupting her thoughts. So she would have to be just that. She might not have his love but she was his wife; she would do all the things expected of her: entertaining, get to know all the right people at the medical school, join all the committees she was asked to, take an interest in local charities, be a good daughter-in-law, and, when he wanted her company, comply willingly.

'Mid-Victorian,' said Matilda loudly to the empty room. 'Only I'm not sitting back and taking it lying down, even if it takes me a lifetime.' He liked her; she was sure of that. He enjoyed her company, they liked doing the same things and they shared a sense of humour; the only thing missing was his love.

She got ready for bed and closed her eyes resolutely. She would begin how she intended to go on; she would go to sleep and not lie awake wondering when he would be home. She didn't hear him come in hours later and make his way to his rooom.

After breakfast she was friendly and suitably quiet while he read his letters, answered his brief remarks with a few placid ones of her own and wished him a pleasant day when he got up to go.

'I'll be home for lunch.' He told her as he went and she said with just the right touch of warmth, 'Oh, good.'

She had post of her own. An invitation to coffee at the medical director's house—a friendly little note from his wife apologising for the short notice but saying that she was anxious that Matilda should meet a few people already known to Rauwerd. There was a letter from Rose, too, asking her to go to lunch in a couple of days' time, and another invitation from a local charity. There was a telephone call after breakfast from Rauwerd's mother asking if they were free to go and see them the following Sunday. Matilda said that she would have to ask Rauwerd, but if he were free, she was sure that they would be delighted.

Quite a good beginning, she decided; the busier her days were, the better. Rauwerd had wanted a wife to come home to, but there wasn't much point in that if he was going to turn tail and rush off to Nikky at the drop of a hat. She must contrive to be away from home from time to time.

She went to the kitchen and consulted with Bep, had a chat with Emma, took the shopping list she was offered and walked to the shops. The list was a short one; she was back with time to spare before setting out for the medical director's house on the other side of the canal.

It was a large, old-fashioned house set in a pleasant garden and close to the medical school. Matilda was ushered into a large drawing-room filled with ladies of all ages. She had expected half-a-dozen fellow visitors and she paused in the doorway, feeling shy. Mevrouw van Kalk surged towards her, a large elderly woman with a kind face, and shook her hand.

'My dear Mevrouw van Kempler, I am so delighted to meet you, Come and be introduced—you know Rauwerd's partners' wives, do you not? Here is Mevrouw Troost, our Senior Medical Officer's wife, and this is ...

The introductions took a long time but once they were over Matilda began to enjoy herself. They were kind, all of them, putting her at her ease and swamping her with invitations to coffee and tea in their own homes. Presently the talk turned to the Spring Ball.

'You will, of course, be coming?' said Mevrouw van Kalk. 'It is a splendid affair and it will be so nice to see Rauwerd partnering his wife at last. We were all beginning to think that he was going to remain a bachelor for the rest of his days.'

Matilda smiled and nodded and answered questions and talked for a while with Beatrix and Marie and Gerda, inviting them to tea. 'Friday?' she wanted to know. 'I have a Dutch lesson in the morning so I shall be able to practise on you all.'

She walked back home and found Rauwerd already there.

'Oh, hello.' She greeted him cheerfully, while her heart thudded against her ribs at the sight of him. 'I'm sorry I wasn't at home. You're early. I've been having a coffee with Mevrouw van Kalk and I met ever so many wives—it'll take me weeks to work off all the invitations to coffee and tea. It was great fun, too. I must work hard at my Dutch. I've a lesson tomorrow. I'll just go and tidy before lunch.'

She skipped away rather breathless, without giving him a chance to get in a word edgeways. But at lunch she asked after his morning, expressed the wish that he would have a good afternoon and mentioned that Rose wanted her to have lunch. 'So you won't mind if I go to Amsterdam?' she asked matter-of-factly. 'Mevrouw van Kalk says there is a splended train service.'

'Jan will drive you; you can phone when you are ready to come back. Taking revenge, Tilly?' He spoke quietly, watching her unsmiling.

It was wonderful how easy it was to conceal one's feelings when one really wanted to. She opened her eyes wide. 'Revenge, Rauwerd? What do you mean? If you don't want me to go to Amsterdam, then I won't.' She gave him a questioning smile.

'By all means go to see Rose. I can't take Dickens with me this afternoon. Would you mind taking him for a walk later on? He is obedient, but perhaps you'd better keep him on a lead.'

'Oh, good, I'd love to. We'll go to the end of Rapenburg and up the other side. Will that be long enough?' She refilled his coffee cup. 'Your mother would like us to visit them on Sunday. I said I'd ask you and ring her back.'

'Lunch? Yes, I'll be free, though I may have to go out on Sunday evening.'

Matilda's insides came to a halt. Nikky again. She said pleasantly, 'Oh, then I'll let her know, shall I?' And then, 'You have so many friends, Rauwerd, and they all have wives; I'm sure I'll never be at a loss for something to do.'

He gave her another keen glance. 'I am glad you are happy, Matilda.'

He got up to go and rather surprisingly dropped a kiss on her cheek as he went.

He was home by five o'clock, a circumstance which gave Matilda great satisfaction, unhappily short-lived, for after less than half an hour's desultory talk he observed that he had several phone calls to make and he went off to his study. Matilda closed the Dutch grammar she had been worrying over with something of a snap and wandered upstairs; it was early to change her dress but she had no intention of sitting there waiting for him to return. She mooned around, discarding first one dress and then another, and finally settled on a silvery grey woollen crêpe, very demure, very becoming and wickedly expensive. The dress

called for extra care with her face and hair and it
wanted but ten minutes to dinner time by the time she
went back to the drawing-room. Rauwerd was there,
sitting in his chair and surprisingly doing nothing. He
got up when she went in and poured her a drink.

'That's a pretty dress,' he commented, and then, 'I
must go out after dinner ... I'm so sorry.'

'You don't have to be sorry,' said Matilda matter-of-
factly. 'I quite understand.'

He raised his eyebrows and although his face was
grave she had the impression that he was secretly
amused. 'Do you? So I don't need to explain?'

'Heavens, no. After all, you explained everything
very clearly before we married.' She gave him a sweet
smile and tossed off her sherry.

Over dinner they discussed giving a dinner party;
the partners and their wives, of course, Rose and
Sybren, Professor Tacx and, it went without saying,
Nikky.

'Next week?' suggested Rauwerd. 'Tuesday? Will
you write the notes and I'll get them posted tomorrow?
Don't forget it's the Spring Ball at the end of next
week, an annual event of some splendour. Get yourself
a new ball gown, Tilly; get Jan to drive you to den
Haag. A pity your car hasn't been delivered yet.'

She made a pleasant rejoinder, poured his coffee and
said equally pleasantly, 'If I'm to write those notes, I'd
better begin straight away. I can do them in English?
Good, then I'll go into the sitting-room. I'll say
goodnight, Rauwerd.'

She had slipped through the door before he could get
to his feet.

The days slid by; everyone accepted for the dinner party and she went to den Haag and spent a good deal of money on a new dress for the ball—satin, the colour of clotted cream, with a wide skirt pleated into a narrow waist and a cunningly cut bodice which showed off her splendid figure to its fullest advantage. She bought matching slippers and a marabou wrap, too, bore them back to the house and didn't mention it to Rauwerd. Hanging the dress in the wardrobe she reflected that normally she would have rushed home and showed Rauwerd the lot, but she doubted sadly if he would be interested.

There was no good wallowing in self-pity. She plunged into the preparations for the dinner party, shared her breakfasts with Rauwerd and took care to be home in the evening when he got back, even though he seldom spent the evenings with her. She was finding her feet, by now, and was acquiring a smattering of Dutch and a casual acquaintance with the wives of Rauwerd's colleagues and friends. She walked Dickens, shopped, took an interest in the running of the house without interfering with Bep, and schooled herself to assume a casual, light-hearted manner when she was with Rauwerd, never asking him where he went or what he did. He was highly thought of in the medical profession, everyone was at pains to tell her so, but since he never mentioned his work other than casually, she didn't ask him about it.

Dressing for the dinner party, she reviewed their married life so far. There was no doubt about them getting on well; they did, but only up to a point. They liked the same things, shared a sense of humour, and,

on the face of things, were a happily married couple; on
the other hand it had been disastrous that she should
have fallen in love with him when all he had to offer was
friendship. Life could be very difficult, thought
Matilda, slipping into the rose-pink dress and clasping
the pearls around her neck, but she had no intention of
giving up hope.

Dinner was a success, even with Nikky there in a
slinky black dress that did nothing for her lack of
curves. Matilda, confident that she looked nice, smiled
and chatted and tried out her Dutch—which pleased
Professor Tacx mightily, even when she said it all
wrong—and received the compliments about her party
with shy dignity. No one hurried away; indeed, they
lingered until almost midnight and, when they left,
reminded her that they would see her at the ball.

She hadn't had much time to talk to Rose. Only as
everyone was getting ready to leave and Nikky said,
'You'll run me back, Rauwerd?' did Sybren, obedient
to his small wife's eloquent eye, say, 'No bother,
Nikky, we'll drop you off. It's not out of our way.'

He clapped Rauwerd on the shoulder in a friendly
fashion, kissed Matilda and swept Nikky out to his car
while Rose kissed Rauwerd and then Matilda. She
didn't say anything, only winked.

Which meant, thought Matilda, standing in the hall
beside Rauwerd, that Rose and Sybren and possibly
any number of the other people knew about Nikky. She
was going to ask Rose next time they met.

Which was at the ball, when, of course, there was no
time for private talk. Matilda, resplendent in the cream
satin, danced the first dance with Rauwerd and after

that didn't see him again until the supper dance when he came to fetch her from a circle of his colleagues who were chatting her up in the nicest possible way.

'What a lovely time I am having; aren't you?' she asked as they went along to the supper room. 'I do like your friends, Rauwerd.

'They appear to like you, my dear. I must say, that dress is quite charming.'

They joined a party of friends for supper and then went back to dance until the small hours. As they circled the floor for the last waltz, Matilda said, 'Shall I ask your mother and father over for lunch in a day or two? I'm sorry they decided not to come, but I'm sure your mother would like to hear about it.'

'And see the dress, of course.'

'Oh, yes. I told her about it, of course, when we went there to lunch.'

He leaned back a little to look at her. 'You didn't tell me, Tilly.'

'Well, I didn't think you'd be interested.' She sounded pleasantly matter-of-fact. 'There are some gorgeous dresses here tonight. It's a very grand affair, isn't it? And I've met a host of new people—there was a nice fat man with a beard . . .'

'The *Burgermeester*, my dear. You've stolen his elderly heart.'

'Oh, good. We'll have him and his wife to dinner, shall we?'

'Aiming to be a prominent hostess, Matilda?' he asked silkily.

She caught her breath with the hurt of it. 'No. I thought that was what you wanted, Rauwerd—

someone to run your house and entertain your friends and be in the house when you get home.'

'Did I say that?'

'Yes. But if you want to ...' She was forced to stop, for the dance was ending and there were people laughing and talking all round them. Nikky was there, of course; she had come with a professor from the university, but there was no sign of him now. Matilda wished her goodnight and saw her join a group of people at the door. She had smiled at Rauwerd and touched his arm as she left them. She was wearing a vivid green sheath with a slashed skirt and long black gloves. Very dramatic.

Matilda fetched her wrap, lingered to speak to the director's wife and went back to the entrance hall. Rauwerd was waiting for her; so was Nikky, cocooned in black fur. Almost everyone else had gone, Rose and Sybren amongst the first; there was only a handful of local people left and no sign of the professor.

'I'll drop you off, Tilly,' said Rauwerd, 'and run Nikky back—Professor Wijse had to leave before the end and she's without transport.'

'Oh, hard luck,' said Matilda. 'Come in and have some coffee first—Bep will have left some ready and it's quite a long drive.'

Nikky gave a girlish laugh. 'Oh, I'll enjoy it, and Rauwerd loves driving at night, don't you?'

Matilda ushered her unwelcome guest into the drawing-room and went along to fetch the coffee. She was crossing the hall with the tray when Rauwerd came in from the car. 'Isn't it rather late?' he asked mildly.

'Well, yes, but it's so late it doesn't matter any more,

does it? Do you have to be at the hospital in the morning?'

He took the tray from her and she sensed his annoyance. 'Yes.'

She made no attempt to hurry over their coffee. Indeed, she engaged Nikky in a rather pointlesss conversation which Rauwerd sat through silently, but at last she put down her cup with a little laugh.

'Oh, dear, I'm half asleep. I'll simply have to go to bed. Do forgive me, Nikky, if I go up now.'

She stood up looking quite superb, her eyes bright and her cheeks flushed, due almost entirely to her smouldering rage. 'I hope we shall see you again soon,' she said insincerely to Nikky. 'It was a delightful evening, wasn't it?'

Rauwerd went to the door and opened it. She paused to whisper, 'I'll say goodnight. There's not much left of it, but I'm sure it will be good!'

She heard his quick furious breath as she swept past him.

Rage and unhappiness upheld her while she undressed and got into bed. Half-way through a sniffing, snuffling weep she fell asleep.

The full horror of what she had done hit her with all its force when she woke. Emma, who had brought her her early morning tea, stared at her face with consternation.

'Miss Tilly, whatever is the matter? Are you ill? Didn't you enjoy the dance?'

Matilda looked at her through red puffy lids. 'It was heavenly, Emma, but I was so tired when we got home . . .'

'Five o'clock I heard the car go round to the garage. The doctor 'as ter go ter work, but you have a nice lie in.'

'I'll feel fine once I'm up, Emma dear, really I will. I'll be down to breakfast as usual.' Five o'clock! It had been three when she had gone to bed.

She felt sick when she contemplated facing Rauwerd presently, which was why she took extra pains with her hair and spent twice as long as usual disguising her pink nose and eyelids. She wore a new outfit, too—a Swiss knitted jacket and skirt with a matching blouse; its bow tied under her chin, which was really rather fetching.

Rauwerd was already at the table, but he got up as he always did, wished her good morning and picked up his letters once more. He looked tired and very stern and the apology which tentatively trembled on her lips was swallowed again; he was still angry. If he had shouted at her, had a blazing row, it would have been easier, but his chilly politeness stifled any wish on her part to apologise. She took a roll and buttered it. She wasn't sorry; he had deserved every word and a great many more besides. She was no man's doormat.

Rauwerd put down the last of his letters and rather disconcertingly sat back in his chair, watching her. 'You have been crying?' he observed and expected an answer.

'I can cry if I wish,' snapped Matilda.

He got up, preparing to go. 'You mustn't over-react, Matilda. I suspect that your imagination is obscuring your common sense; it is certainly blinding you to the obvious.' He stopped by her chair, looking down at her unsmiling. 'We must have a talk, you and I. I hadn't

intended to say anything yet—after all, we have been
married such a short time.'

'You're angry?' she muttered, not looking at him.

'Yes. I won't be home for lunch ...'

'If there are any calls for you ...'

'I shall be over at the hospital,' he said and added
silkily, 'not in Amsterdam!'

He whistled to Dickens and went away leaving her to
stare at her plate while she fought terror, and tears.

It wouldn't do to mope. She drank several cups of
coffee and went to discuss the day's meals with Bep.
Bep wanted to know all about the ball and so did
Emma, so Matilda sat down at the kitchen table and
described as many dresses as she could remember and
what they had eaten for supper. Only when the two
ladies were satisfied that they knew everything there
was to know, was she able to talk about food. If
Rauwerd was going to quarrel with her she would feel
sick; she chose a meal which made that prospect less
likely, made her shopping list, donned a smart little felt
hat and gloves, and, armed with a basket and her purse,
set off to the shops.

It was a chilly morning and windy and the town was
busy. She stopped to examine the fruit at her favourite
stall just outside the supermarket and actually had an
orange in her hand when the bomb concealed in the
shop exploded.

CHAPTER EIGHT

MATILDA felt herself tossed into the air and then fall, half smothered in oranges, apples and cabbages. Her fall was cushioned by a large crate of tomatoes which puréed themselves all over her person and from which, after the first shocked seconds, she dragged herself upright. The stall's owner was half buried under a mound of potatoes and Matilda dragged her from them, aware of the profound silence almost at once broken by cries and screams and moans from inside the supermarket. It astonished her that she was still clutching her basket and purse; she looked at them in a silly kind of way for a moment and then handed them shakily to the stallholder.

The police and ambulances and fire engines would arrive within minutes; in the meantime there was surely something she could do to help. She picked her way over the debris around her and edged into the supermarket. Its front had been blown out and the floor was knee-deep in tins and broken glass, broken bags of rice and sugar, tea and flour; from the depths of its interior people were staggering, calling to each other, crying for help. She pushed past them; the bomb had gone off somewhere at the back of the store and that was where the injured would be.

There was smoke and dust so that she couldn't see very well, and shelves still tumbling lazily to the ground, carrying their contents with them, making progress difficult. She began to come across the injured then, lying silent, some of them pinned to the ground by falling masonry, others were wandering around in a dazed way, seemingly unaware of their wounds. Matilda, still dazed herself, began to work her way from one victim to the next, doing what she could, which wasn't much, uttering reassuring words, straightening broken arms and legs as gently as she could, pulling away the more easily moved debris, snatching a handful of dusty tea-towels on sale on the shelves still standing and using them to cover the more obvious wounds.

She was joined almost at once by two policemen and three men who had followed them in, and her nurse's training automatically took over. She began to look more carefully at the wounded lying around groaning, mostly women, and she made sure that they could be carried out without more damage being done. More men were making their way towards them now and she was dimly aware of ambulance bells and a good deal of shouting. She felt light-headed but there wasn't time to think about that; some of the people lying there were severely wounded, even dead; they had to be got to hospital as soon as possible. She crawled to a young woman lying unconscious under a pile of milk cartons and began to fling them aside. It was a good thing she was unconscious for she had lost an arm . . . Matilda did what she could with her remaining tea-towel and watched while one of the men picked the girl up and carried her away.

'*Vlug*,' cried Matilda, thankfully recalling her Dutch

lessons, although anyone in their senses would have known that quickness was of the essence. And then, as she caught sight of a battered pushchair and a small child still strapped into it, 'Oh, someone come quickly . . .'

One of the policemen heard her and made his way to her side. Together they pulled the child clear just as the first of the ambulancemen arrived. A mound of tins had fallen in a great heap between the shelves; Matilda could hear cries from beneath it and began burrowing frantically towards the sound.

'Over here,' she called urgently, but the hubbub was considerable by now, with a great many helpers all willing but lacking someone to organise them. The ambulancemen were too busy getting victims into the ambulances; the police were hampered by frantic people searching for children and friends. She tugged at the end of a broken shelf and a few dozen tins rolled away leaving a gap with an arm sticking out from it. She edged forward, took it in her hand and squeezed it gently and was rewarded by an answering squeeze. She began to move the tins carefully and presently was rewarded by the sight of a face, dirty and pale but alive. She paused for a moment and said joyfully, 'Oh, hello.' The face stretched into a smile although the voice was too faint to hear. Matilda smiled back and began, very carefully, to move the tins.

At the hospital the bomb had, naturally enough, taken everybody by surprise. Rauwerd, at his desk after a busy outpatients' session had lifted the receiver before the last rumbles had died away.

'Yes, a bomb,' agreed the medical director, 'or a gas explosion.' The rescue team was to be ready in five minutes. 'Deal with the situation as you think fit, Rauwerd—you're free?'

The team was alerted. Rauwerd had scarcely put down the phone when there was a call from the police. 'Give us five minutes. Much damage?'

He dialled again and, when Jan answered, 'Is *Mevrouw* at home?' He sounded calm and unhurried, it was Jan who sounded worried.

'She left about twenty minutes ago to go to the shops. Shall I look for her? We all three could go ...'

'I'm on my way there, Jan. Stay at home and ask Bep and Emma to get things ready in case she has been hurt. Does she shop at the supermarket?'

'Almost never, Doctor.'

'That's where the bomb exploded, Jan, so there is a good chance she's all right.'

He rang off and got into his white coat and went to join the team and the waiting ambulances.

'The supermarket,' he told them. 'Get the ambulance as near as you can and split into teams of three. I'll go in ahead of you with Cor and Wim.' He nodded to the two young housemen standing by him. 'The rest of you follow as we've done in practices.'

It was no distance, a matter of a minute or two, but they were hindered by the people milling around; the police ahead of them cleared a path and the ambulances stopped, unable to get nearer for the rubble in the street. The fire engines had come in from the opposite end, and the police were urging people to stay away so that the rescue work could go ahead.

Rauwerd, making his way over fallen masonry and glass and ruined stalls, saw that there was already a row of victims lying in the cleared space outside the supermarket. He said over his shoulder, 'Tell the second team to organise stretchers and get these people back to the hospital.' He noted the tea towels. 'They've had a very rough and ready first aid.' He switched on his walkie-talkie to warn the hospital and ducked into the dust and smoke of the ruined store.

Matilda was moving the tins very carefully and slowly. The pallor of the face visible in their midst urged her to fling them aside as fast as she could go, but that might bring a cascade on to the owner of the face. She needed help but although there were people round her now, struggling to free the victims, they had their own worries. She didn't allow her despair to show on her face, however, for the sickly white face peering back at her was looking anxious.

'Not long now,' said Matilda with pseudo-cheerfulness. Her hands were cut and bleeding and she was covered in a fine dust which had stuck to the squashed fruit and veg still adhering to her person. She felt dizzy, too, and every now and again her surroundings dipped and swayed around her but she kept doggedly on.

The sight of her, with her hair hanging in a dusty cloud around her shoulders, a trickle of dried blood on one cheek and what looked like the beginnings of a black eye, brought Rauwerd up short. He said, 'Oh, my dear Tilly, thank God you are safe. You're not hurt?'

He had caught her by the arm and she looked up into his face, white and etched with lines she had never seen before. She said in a tightly controlled voice, for she felt rather peculiar, 'Are you the rescue team? How did you know I was here?'

'I didn't—I just hoped that you were all right and safe.'

'Well, I am, but we must get this poor soul out—all these tins,' she cried distractedly.

He shouted to one of the team members and, taking no notice of her protests, sat her down on an upturned shelf. 'Don't move, Tilly,' he told her and although he spoke quietly she didn't dare disobey him.

An ambulanceman joined them and carefully and slowly they eased out the owner of the face, laid her on a stretcher and carried her away.

'And now you,' said Rauwerd. 'You're to go back with one of the team and be taken home, and don't argue, please, Tilly.'

Something in his voice stopped her from protesting and indeed there was nothing she wanted more than to be at home, in bed, asleep. Rauwerd hauled her gently to her feet and handed her over to a policeman, then immediately turned his attention to the latest victim to be carried out of the ruins around him.

She felt a flash of utter misery that he could do that as she was led away, the policeman's sturdy arm hooked into hers. She was glad of it; once she could get into the street away from the dust and smoke and pitiful cries for help she would feel better.

They were almost at the ruined entrance when her legs turned to cotton wool and she keeled over, to be caught before she reached the ground and carried to one of the police cars. Her companion had seen the doctor's face as he had turned away. The doctor had had to stay, poor devil, thought the policeman, so it behoved him to take care of this pretty English girl who had been so quick to give help. He eased her into the nearest police car and told the driver to go to the hospital. 'And make it quick.'

Matilda, coming to as she was put on a stretcher in the first-aid department, shook the policeman's hand and muttered, '*Dank U*,' and even managed a smile. She added. 'The doctor . . .' and stopped, at a loss for words.

'I tell him,' said her kind companion.

The Medical Director came himself to look her over. 'Nothing serious,' he assured her. 'An ATS injection, and a nurse will clean up those cuts and scratches. You're going to have a black eye but there's no concussion. I hear that you were one of the first to give aid.' He patted her hand. 'We are all very proud of you. I'm so glad Rauwerd found you; he was anxious.'

She nodded, furious with herself that she couldn't stop the tears trickling down her dirty cheeks.

'So he knows you are safe. Now we'll see to you and send you home to bed, and that's an order, Matilda.'

Her hands were scratched and torn, she was grazed, and her eye was rapidly turning a rich purple. She was cleaned up, had her injection and was driven home, where she had a rapturous welcome from Bep, Emma and Jan.

'The doctor told us to have everything ready in case you had been hurt,' said Emma. 'You're to have a bath and go to bed. That worried he was, too,' Emma tut-

tutted. 'Them nasty old bombs, scaring the wits out of decent folks.'

Matilda, bathed, her hair washed, and made to drink hot milk, got into bed, closed her one good eye, and was asleep instantly.

It was well into the afternoon when the last of the victims had been taken from the ruins and the rescue team had gone wearily back to the hospital, before Rauwerd opened his own front door. Jan, hovering at the back of the hall, heard him.

'You're back, doctor. Coffee? A meal? *Mevrouw* is sleeping.'

'Coffee, please, Jan. I'll change my clothes—I've cleaned up at the hospital, but I need another suit. I must go back at once.' He started up the stairs. 'I'll take a look at my wife.'

Matilda was curled up into a ball, her sore hands stretched out on the coverlet, her eye, swollen and richly purple, half hidden by her hair. The faithful Dickens, keeping her company by the bed, got up as Rauwerd stood looking down at her; there was a look on the doctor's weary face which, if she could have seen it, would have made the black eye worthwhile. But she didn't stir as he bent and kissed her gently and went along to his own room, taking Dickens with him.

She woke at the end of the afternoon, drank the tea Bep brought her and decided to get up. She felt fine except for the eye and her hands and Rauwerd would soon be home. She put on one of her pretty dresses, tied her hair back with a ribbon because her hands were too clumsy to put it up, and went downstairs, closely shadowed by her faithful household.

The phone had been ringing all day, Jan informed her, and it rang again while he was telling her this. It was Rose, her pretty voice anxious.

'Tilly? You're all right? Sybren drove over to Leiden as soon as he heard about the bomb. He saw Rauwerd just for a moment—he was up to his eyes, of course, and so dreadfully worried about you because he'd had to leave you, but he couldn't do anything else, could he, being in charge of the rescue team? Have you seen him since?'

'No, I've been asleep. He came back to change his clothes but he didn't wake me. He'll be back any minute . . .'

'Oh, Tilly, I'm so relieved that it wasn't worse for you. Sybren says everyone is talking about the way you waded in and helped and gave first aid. Will you feel like having me to tea in a day or two and telling me all about it?'

'Oh, Rose, I'd love that—what about tomorrow?'

'Lovely. May I bring little Sybren with me?'

She put down the receiver and Jan appeared at her side. 'May I suggest a nice glass of sherry, *Mevrouw*? The doctor would like you to have it.'

He handed her a glass. 'There are flowers, also—from the director's wife and the partners' wives and from Professor Tacx. May I say how proud we are of you, *Mevrouw*?' He beamed at her, picking his words carefully so as to get the English right.

'Why, thank you, Jan, but there were other people helping, too, you know. And it was lovely to come home to you all here.' She glanced at the clock. 'I wonder when the doctor will be back.'

'You would like me to telephone?'

'No, I don't think so, Jan. They must be very busy. I don't know how many people were hurt, though I dare say quite a few were transferred to Amsterdam or den Haag. Could Bep put dinner back for half an hour?'

'Certainly, *Mevrouw*.'

But the half-hour came and went and in the end she dined alone. It was almost ten o'clock when she heard his voice as he spoke to Jan in the hall and whistled to Dickens.

'You should be in bed,' he said from the hall, and he spoke so harshly that she felt the silly, easy tears prick her eyelids.

'Hello, Rauwerd.' Her voice came out expressionless. 'I slept well all day, thank you. Would you like dinner? Bep's got everything ready for you.'

He had come right into the room and she looked at him now. He looked tired to death; she longed to push him into his chair and throw her arms round his neck and hug him and fuss around him with a drink and his supper, while he unburdened himself of his day's work, as any husband would.

Only he wasn't any husband; he was Rauwerd, who had no intention of doing anything of the sort.

'How do you feel?' he wanted to know. 'Is that eye painful?' He sat down opposite her. 'Van Kalk examined you thoroughly; you escaped lightly.'

'Yes, didn't I? Were the casualties high?'

He nodded. 'We've transferred about half of them; there are several in intensive care, though.'

'It was dreadful. You must be very tired. Did you tell Jan that you wanted a meal? I'll go and see ...'

'He's bringing me some coffee and sandwiches.'

'I'll get you a drink.'

'Stay where you are, I can get it. By the way, a woman called at the hospital; she was the stallholder where you were standing. Says you were so kind and helpful when you were both knocked over. She found your handbag and returned it; it's in the hall, rather the worse for wear, I'm afraid. You are by way of being a heroine, Tilly.'

'That's nonsense—I was a bit nearer the store than anyone else, that's all.'

He said, 'You might have been killed, or mutilated.' His voice was harsh again. Jan came in then, which was a pity, for Matilda had hoped that he would say more.

But what was there to say? He wasn't a man to pretend to feelings he didn't have for her and she didn't blame him for that. She poured his coffee and watched him eat the sandwiches, and although she longed to talk she held her tongue. She gave him a second cup of coffee and when he had drunk it he fell asleep.

He woke after half an hour. 'My dear Tilly, I'm so sorry. You should have wakened me ...'

She said in a motherly voice, 'Why? You need a nap. I think you should go to bed at once. I suppose you have to go to the hospital in the morning?'

'Yes.' He was staring at her and she met his gaze with her one good eye.

'I am proud of you, Tilly, and there has been no chance to tell you so. I was so scared and when I saw you there, quite oblivious of your danger, I said nothing. I hope you'll forgive me for that.'

She got out of her chair. 'Well, of course I do. There

was no chance to talk, was there? And I didn't expect
you to bother with me when there were people lying
around crying for help. I'm going to bed.' She smiled at
him. 'It's been quite a day, hasn't it?'

He went to the door with her and opened it.

'Oh, your father phoned this evening just to make
quite sure that we were all right. I missed his first
two calls but Jan coped marvellously. Goodnight,
Rauwerd.'

She got up as usual in the morning to find that
Rauwerd had already left for the hospital, leaving a
message with Jan that he thought it unlikely that he
would be home for lunch.

The morning was largely taken up with answering
the telephone calls. It astonished Matilda that there
were so many of them, but then, of course, Rauwerd
was well known in the town. Dickens had been left at
home, so she donned the eyepatch Rauwerd had left for
her and took him for a brisk walk along Rapenburg and
then submitted to the anxious attentions of Emma and
Bep, eating the lunch they had made with such care
although she wasn't in the least hungry and then going
to the sitting-room to wait for Rose.

It was quiet there and the sun shining through the
window gave out a pleasant warmth. She curled up in a
chair with Dickens beside her and closed her eyes.
Rauwerd would be working and there would be no let
up for a few days to come. Perhaps when things had got
back to normal she would be able to persuade him to
take a few days off. Go over to England, perhaps, and
see a play, or just laze around in his London home or
walk in one of the parks.

She was almost asleep when Jan came in and said apologetically, 'Juffrouw van Wijk is here, *Mevrouw*, and she insists on seeing you.'

Matilda sat up straight and assumed an expression of pleased surprise. Just in time.

Nikky pushed past Jan and didn't wait for him to close the door before she said, 'I thought Rauwerd would be here—I came to see him, really. My God, what a fearful shock I had when I heard. He's not hurt? I phoned the hospital but they didn't know where he was; nor did that man of yours when I telephoned yesterday. This morning I was told that he was unable to answer the telephone—I could leave a message for him with his secretary.' She laughed rather wildly. 'His secretary! If he'd known it was I, he would have answered the phone.'

Matilda heard her out and then said politely, 'Do sit down. And do tell me, why should Rauwerd have answered your telephone call? He is a doctor, and they are working almost round the clock at the hospital.'

Nikky fixed her with an angry look. 'Oh, you don't know what you're talking about.' She burst into sudden laughter. 'Oh, poor Matilda, your eye—you do look a fright—and your hands. You look as though you've been scrubbing floors for years. You won't be able to go anywhere for days. Not that it would matter; you don't go out together, do you? I mean, the two of you for fun?' She leaned back in her chair. 'Rauwerd and I always had fun; he'd die of boredom if he didn't have me to visit. Does he tell you he's working late?'

Matilda sat like a ramrod, very pale, her eyes sparkling with rage. Any minute now she knew she would say something rash, or slap Nikky's face. Neither of them had heard Jan answer the door and admit Rose, who was standing at the door Jan had half opened, shamelessly listening.

She flung it wide now and went in, the carrycot dangling from one hand.

'Tilly, dear, how lovely to see you.' She turned an enquiring face towards Nikky. 'Oh, hello. Just going, are you? Jan's in the hall; he'll see you out, and don't you dare to say another word.'

She stood back by the open door and Jan, who had heard every word, went to the front door and held it wide. Rose was small and unassuming but she had a way with her; Nikky went. Slowly, it was true, but she went.

Rose put the carrycot down on the sofa and sat down on the arm of Matilda's chair. Matilda was paper white and tears of rage were trickling down her cheeks. Her pallor threw her black eye into violent relief and she was shaking. Presently she said, 'Thank you, Rose. I couldn't think of anything to say, you know. I just wanted to hit her. She said . . . Did you hear?'

'Oh, yes,' said Rose comfortably. 'I was standing at the door, listening to every word.'

'Rose, is it true? I mean about her and Rauwerd? Will you tell me?'

Rose said carefully, 'She wanted him—he's quite a catch, you know. She never loved him, only his name and his money and the prestige his work gives him— and I'm quite sure that Rauwerd never considered marrying her, didn't even fall in love with her; he just tolerated her because he's a kind man. No one likes her and I suppose because of that he was her friend. Ask him, Tilly. He'll tell you that Nikky isn't of any importance to him.'

Matilda sniffed, blew her nose and mopped her face. 'Heavens, you must think I'm a silly fool to take any notice of the woman. I'll—I'll have a talk with Rauwerd.'

'You do that. You see, everything will be all right. That's a really lovely eye. Were you terrified?'

'Petrified. It's like being turned to stone for a few moments; you can't move or speak. I ruined a new suit, too.'

'Plenty more where that came from,' said Rose cheerfully. 'I say, I'm sorry I was so high-handed just now, ordering Nikky out of your house, only you looked as though you were going to thump her.'

'I was. I wish I had, too.' They giggled together. 'Oh, good, here's Jan with our tea. Is the baby all right there? He's very quiet . . .'

'Asleep,' said his proud mother. 'He's so placid, bless him. When's the next Dutch lesson? Isn't Professor Tacx a nice old man?'

Emma and Bep had provided a lovely tea: tiny sandwiches, scones, toasted and buttered, rich chocolate cake and wafer-thin bread and butter. They took their time over it and hadn't finished when Rauwerd came in.

He kissed them both, studied his small godson and sat down by the fire. When Jan came in with fresh tea Matilda gave him a cup and asked. 'Is it still very busy on the ward? Are the patients recovering?'

He studied her face; tears and rage had taken their

toll but her voice was quietly enquiring. 'Ordered chaos is the term; we've borrowed nurses from here and there and, of course, it took them a little time to find their way around. But the patients are coming along nicely. Some nasty injuries and still three in intensive care.' He had demolished the rest of the bread and butter and was starting on the cake. Matilda wondered if had had lunch, and put the plate of scones within his reach. He ate thooo, too, while he carried on desultory conversation until Rose got up to go.

'And may I just ring Sybren,' she asked, 'to let him know that I'm on my way?' When she had done that and kissed Matilda she asked Rauwerd, 'Will you carry the baby down to the car for me?'

With the infant safely stowed in the back of the car she paused as he opened the car door for her. 'Look, this isn't my business and probably you'll never speak to me again, but there is something I must say ...'

'About Tilly?' His voice was very quiet.

She nodded. 'Nikky van Wijk was here when I arrived. She just walked in—she wasn't asked. I don't know what she said before I arrived but she was saying a whole lot—I stood at the door and listened—lies about you and her. But there were little bits of truth mixed in and it all sounded plausible.' She looked rather anxiously at his face; he was angry but there was something besides anger in his tired face.

'You're furious. I'm sorry if you don't want to be friends any more.'

He smiled faintly. 'Yes, I'm furious, but not with you, Rose, or with Tilly. I promise you I will do something to put matters right.' He bent and kissed her again. 'Sybren's a lucky fellow.'

She beamed at him. 'Yes, isn't he? I shall tell him all this. Will you mind?'

'I should find it extraordinary if you didn't—you're too close for secrets, aren't you?' He shut the door on her. 'Drive carefully.'

Rauwerd didn't sit down when he went back into the sitting-room; he went to stand at the window, looking out into the garden, but he turned around when Matilda spoke. She had had time to think what she was going to say and to school her voice to matter-of-factness.

'Nikky called this afternoon. She was worried about you. She phoned yesterday but Jan didn't know where you were and I was asleep. She tried the hospital, too, and again today; they told her that you were unable to take calls but she didn't believe them so she came here.'

'And what did she have to say?' His look was so intent that she glanced away.

'Well, she was upset, naturally . . .'

He sauntered towards her. 'Why naturally, Tilly?'

She hesitated. 'You're old friends—— She—she has a great regard for you.'

'What a nice way of putting it. And do you believe that?'

Matilda met his gaze squarely. 'No, but I don't think it matters what I think. Rose came just before Nikky left; she told me to ask you . . . But I don't think I want to know. I'd like to forget it; it isn't as though . . .' She paused. 'I expect you would like to go and see Nikky; she was very upset.'

He lounged against a chair but now he straightened

up. 'Why, I do believe I'll do just that, Matilda.' He had come to stand in front of her, hands in his pockets. 'You are almost too good to be true, you know, although, of course that should be easy since your own feelings aren't involved. You are also as blind as a bat.' He went briskly to the door. 'Don't wait dinner for me,' he said cheerfully as he went out.

She went to bed shortly after dinner with the excuse that she had a headache, and certainly her eye bore out evidence of the statement. She was sitting up in bed knitting with a kind of concentrated fury when there was a tap on her door and Rauwerd came in.

'Emma says you have a headache.' He took her wrist in his hand. 'Your pulse is fast; do you not feel well, Matilda? You have had a bad time, you know.' He looked at her with narrowed eyes. 'Or have you a headache?'

'No, I haven't. I said I had otherwise Emma and Bep would have wondered why I came to bed so early.'

'And why did you?' He sat down on the side of the bed and took the knitting out of her hands.

She shook her head. 'I thought I felt tired, but once I was in bed I wasn't.' She smiled at him with determined brightness, suddenly certain that he had something to tell her. He had been to see Nikky and they would have talked, about her probably.

'I'm going over to London on Sunday to give details of the bombing to a committee of hospital authorities and discuss the nature of the injuries. I have two consultations as well. I shall be there for three days, and I'd like you to come with me, Tilly. We will go to the house in Tilden Street, of course. You could shop if you wish and we might go to a show.'

She studied his face; it gave nothing away. She asked slowly, 'Does Nikky know?'

She wished she knew what he was thinking; his face was so still and his eyes half closed.

'Yes.'

She said wearily. 'And I suppose, when we're there, I stay and you come back here—there are all sorts of excuses you could make.'

His voice was so cold that she actually shivered at the sound of it. 'You think that? You must be out of your mind, Matilda.' He got up from the bed and stood towering over her.

'Well, I'm not,' said Matilda, 'not any more. And I won't go with you.' She pulled the bedclothes over her ears. 'Take Nikky,' she added into the pillows. But he hadn't heard that. He was already out of the room, closing the door with a deliberate quietness which was much worse than a resounding slam.

Because she lay awake until the small hours, she overslept. Rauwerd had already gone to the hospital by the time she got down and Jan told her, with a shake of his head, that he wouldn't be back until the early evening.

'The doctor is working too hard,' he told her, 'and now he goes to London.'

He cast a quick glance at Matilda's face. 'You will be staying here, *Mevrouw*? The doctor says that you are still not quite well.' He gave her a fatherly smile. 'We must all take care of you.'

She murmured suitably, feeling guilty, nibbled at her breakfast and had a long conversation on the phone with her mother-in-law.

'Rauwerd phoned this morning, my dear ; such a pity you aren't well enough to go to London with him, it would have made a pleasant little break for you both, but you are wise to stay at home after such an ordeal.'

Matilda, feeling guiltier than ever, invited her in-laws to lunch the Sunday after Rauwerd got back, and hung up, to plunge into a variety of small chores to keep her busy. She was dreading Rauwerd's return ; indeed, she felt sick whenever she thought about it. Unnecessarily so, as it turned out, for he was his usual coolly pleasant self and no mention was made of their conversation on the previous evening, nor of his trip to London.

The five days till Sunday dragged by. A number of people called to see how she was. Rose telephoned and wisely said nothing at all about Rauwerd, only made a date for the following week and Matilda went to two meetings of charities she had been asked to patronise, the black patch covering her eye which was now yellow and green as well as purple. On Sunday, early, Rauwerd left for London.

CHAPTER NINE

SUNDAY stretched endlessly before Matilda. She and Rauwerd had bidden each other a polite goodbye after breakfast and she had watched him drive away, wishing with her whole heart that she was with him. If he had given the smallest sign that he wished for her company she would have begged his pardon and got into the car just as she was. But he had given no indication of regret at going alone. She watched the Rolls slide away and when it was out of sight, went indoors, got her coat and took Dickens for a long walk. She ate her solitary lunch under the kindly eye of Jan, and then spent the afternoon in the garden, weeding, with Dickens keeping patiently to her side. Rauwerd's mother and father were coming to tea; they were a welcome break in her lonely day and she listened eagerly to his mother's tales of his boyhood and proud reminiscences of his success as a medical student.

'He works too hard,' said his fond parent, 'but, of course, you can understand that, my dear, being a nurse yourself.' She peered closely at Matilda's wan countenance. 'I must say you have been badly shaken; you are far too pale and heavy-eyed. When Rauwerd gets back he must take a few days off and take you somewhere quiet. You'll know of his small farm in Friesland, but of course he has had no chance to take you there yet. It will be ideal for you both.'

Matilda made a suitable reply; it was the first time she had heard about a farm, but then there was so much she didn't know about Rauwerd. She doubted very much if he would wish to take her there. They saw little enough of each other; to be together on a farm miles from nowhere, as it probably was, didn't seem a good idea.

When her guests had gone she took Dickens for another walk, presently ate dinner and then went back to sit in the sitting-room with her knitting. But she allowed it to rest in her lap, not attempting to do a stitch of it. She had had time to think during the day and she knew what she was going to do. She was going to see Nikky and find out the truth for herself. She had been cowardly, ignoring a situation which had been bound to worsen, and which had. There was a second car in the garage, a small Daimler; when Jan came in to see if she wanted anything, she voiced her intention of driving to Amsterdam in the morning. But Jan was unexpectedly firm about this. With all due respect, he was quite certain that the doctor would be most uneasy if she were to drive herself. Her own car would arrive shortly and no doubt the doctor would take her for several drives to make sure that she perfectly understood the slightly different rules of the road in Holland. He pretended not to see her quick frown, and went on, 'If *Mevrouw* will allow me, I will drive you myself, wait for as long as you wish, and bring you back home.'

He looked at her almost pleadingly and she saw no alternative.

'Well, thank you, Jan, if that will make you easier. I intend to visit Juffrouw van Wijk. I don't know where she lives, but I expect I can find it in the telephone book.'

'Juffrouw van Wijk has a flat close to the Leidse Plein, *Mevrouw*. I will drive you there and park close by until you are ready to return.'

'Oh, will you, Jan? Thank you. I don't suppose I shall be long. If we got there at about ten-thirty tomorrow morning?'

'Very good, *Mevrouw*. You will be home for lunch? So that I can tell Bep?'

'Oh, yes. I—I—haven't any plans.'

Which wasn't quite true. Her head seethed with them, most of them highly impracticable. She sat back and thought out what she wanted to say to Nikky. If Nikky would see her . . .

She took great pains with her appearance in the morning. The fine wool suit was a perfect fit and her shoes, elegant and high-heeled, matched her clutch bag. She had been uncertain about a hat but finally decided that it might make her feel that much more self-confident. It was head-hugging with a stiffened bow at the back and gave her, she hoped, dignity, a commodity she was determined to keep at all costs that morning.

There was a lot of traffic and she was secretly relieved that Jan drove and not she, for Nikky lived in the heart of the city, down a narrow street lined by solid square houses, all of them converted into flats.

Jan drew up half-way down the street and helped her out. 'There's a line of meters just round the corner, *Mevrouw*,' he told her. 'I'll leave the car and stroll around until you are ready. I'll not be far away and I'll keep the block in sight.'

'What good care you take of me, Jan.' She paused on the pavement to smile at him.

'A pleasure, *Mevrouw*. Besides, I had my orders from the doctor to look after you.'

Matilda paused on the pavement; just for a moment she faltered. If Rauwerd knew what she was doing . . . She could see his face very vividly in her mind's eye, white and angry, his eyes like blue stones. She gave herself a little shake; angry or not, she was hopelessly in love with him. There would never be anyone else for her, she was sure of that, but if Nikky had spoken the truth . . . But that was why she was there, wasn't it? So that she could find out for herself? She reached the entrance and marched in, found Nikky's name on the cards against the neat row of bells, pressed the second one down and went briskly upstairs. The first floor had four front doors; Nikky opened hers as Matilda lifted her hand to the knocker.

She was surprised, and just for the moment bereft of words, which gave Matilda the chance to say with polite firmness, 'I'd like to talk to you, if I may, just for a little while—about you and Rauwerd.'

Just for a moment she thought that Nikky was going to slam the door in her face, but then she said sullenly, 'Oh, come in then . . .'

They went into a sitting-room, modern and sparsely furnished with uncomfortable-looking chairs, a coffee-table of mirror glass and some impressionist paintings on the scarlet-papered walls. Not a room to relax in, but then she didn't want to relax. She sat down gingerly on the least uncomfortable chair.

'I'd like the truth about you and Rauwerd. I don't mean just bits and pieces of it, or what you choose to tell me. Are you in love with him?'

Nikky laughed. 'Lord no, nor could ever be, but he's got everything a woman wants, hasn't he? Good looks, money—heaps of it—a life-style to please any girl and highly thought of in his work. He was—how do you say—just my cup of tea.'

'And does he love you? Or did he ever love you?'

'You're a silly kind of woman, aren't you? Of course he didn't and he doesn't. We have known each other for years. I suppose, because I was alone and didn't get asked out much, he took pity on me. If he'd asked me to marry him I would have done, make no mistake about that. But he didn't. He married you. I suppose I hated you, so I decided to have another try at getting him away from you. Only I didn't succeed, did I? You know that he came to see me? Well, that's the end of a beautiful friendship—I'm off to the States. I know a few people there; American men are supposed to be good husbands ... I shall miss him, though, always ready to sort things out for me, give me lifts, lend me money, but nothing more than that.'

She had been standing by the wide picture window; now she came and sat down opposite Matilda. 'Do you believe me? Why didn't you ask Rauwerd?'

'No, I couldn't do that. You see, if he had loved you and you loved him, then I would have had to do something about it, wouldn't I? I'd like him to be happy more than anything else in the world.' She paused. 'And yes, I do believe you.'

'You're in love with him, aren't you?'

'Yes.' Matilda got to her feet. 'Thank you for seeing me. I hope you'll be happy in America.'

'Happy?' Nikky asked mockingly. 'Oh, yes, though not your idea of happy—Sunday lunch with mother-in-law, and a pack of children round your feet, and Rauwerd's slippers put to warm each evening.'

There was no suitable answer to that; Matilda went to the door and made her escape.

Jan was waiting. She got back into the car and he turned it and began on the drive back. After a few minutes she asked, 'Jan, I want to go over to London. Can I phone for a place on a flight tomorrow morning?'

'Indeed you can, *Mevrouw*. I'll see to it for you if you will tell me when you want to go, and I can drive you to Schiphol. Would you wish to let the doctor know?'

She felt a gathering excitement inside her. 'No, thank you, Jan. I'd like to surprise him. If I could get a flight about eleven o'clock, I'd be at the house by about two, wouldn't I?'

Back in Leiden again, she had a belated cup of coffee and took Dickens for a walk. She would have liked to have rehearsed exactly what she was going to say to Rauwerd, but her thoughts were too chaotic. She only knew that she would have to apologise before embarking on explanations. She walked along the deserted street, her head in the clouds, while Dickens trotted beside her. She walked until she was tired and then went back for lunch, a meal which Bep served almost an hour late without saying a word.

Jan had booked her a seat on a flight just before midday and she spent a good deal of the afternoon curled up in a chair in the drawing-room wondering what Rauwerd was doing, still trying to think of what she would say when she saw him again. She wandered up to her room presently and went through her wardrobe, deciding what she would wear, and then packing a small overnight bag. She washed her hair and did her nails and went down to eat a dinner she didn't want. She wouldn't sleep a wink, she was sure, but the moment she laid her head on the pillow she did so, and only wakened when Emma came in with her morning tea.

You'll be coming back with the doctor?' Emma wanted to know.

'Oh, dear Emma, yes. That'll be tomorrow evening late or the following morning. I'm not quite sure.' She bounced up in bed. 'And Emma, if Mevrouw van Kempler phones, will you tell her that I'm in England and we'll both be back in day or two. I'll telephone her as soon as we get home.'

Emma studied her with a speculative eye. 'I must say you look 'appy, Miss Tilly, though that's as it should be, you and the doctor being man and wife. It's not right for yer to be apart, when all's said and done.'

The plane was full and at Heathrow it took a long time to get through Customs, even though she had no luggage. She found a taxi at length and was driven to Tilden Street. But that took time, too, what with heavy traffic and a delay because of an accident ahead of them.

It was getting on for three o'clock by the time she opened the door of the house in the quiet street near Grosvenor Square, to be met in the hall by Cribbs's dignified, 'Madam, this is a pleasant surprise. Have you had lunch? Perhaps a cup of tea?' He beamed at her with real pleasure. 'You are quite recovered? The doctor said that you had had a bad time of it.'

'I'm fine, thank you, Cribbs. Is—is the doctor at home?'

He shook his head. 'No, madam, he left this morning early to go to some meeting or other, and then he said that he would go on to the hospital—he had two or three appointments there, I understand, and he didn't expect to be back much before this evening.'

Her disappointment was so great that she had to swallow back her tears. But she hadn't come all this way to be put off so easily.

'I'll go over to the hospital, Cribbs. The doctor might be free earlier than he thought. Is he dining at home?'

'Yes, madam. I believe he intended to go back to Leiden tomorrow evening; he didn't know for certain.'

Her one thought was to go to Rauwerd at once, but common sense took over. 'I'd love a cup of tea, Cribbs, and I'm just going upstairs to tidy myself.'

She did her face with great care and brushed her hair until it shone and then wound it neatly, determined to look her best. When she went downstairs Mrs Cribbs had added a plate of dainty sandwiches to the tea tray. Sitting in the taxi Cribbs had called for her, Matilda felt ready for anything.

The hospital entrance hall was empty, save for the porter in his little box. Matilda poked her head through its window before she had time to get scared. 'I want to see Dr van Kempler,' she told him in what she hoped was an assured voice. 'I'm his wife.'

The porter put down his paper and looked her over

slowly. 'Does he expect you, ma'am?'

'Well, no ...'

'He'll be at the meeting then ... began at three o'clock and likely to last for an hour or two. Can't interrupt it, I'm afraid.'

'Oh. Well, can I wait here?'

He said grudgingly, 'I suppose you could. Maybe he'll not be so long. There's no telling.' He nodded towards the back of the hall. 'There's a bench there, between those two statues.'

Matilda thanked him politely although she was bursting with impatience. The seat was hard and cold and not easily seen by those who passed to and fro through the hall. Each time she heard footsteps she looked up eagerly, but there was no sign of Rauwerd. Fewer and fewer people passed by and presently, weary from excitement and anxiety, she closed her eyes.

When she opened them the place was deserted; even the usual hospital noises were hushed. She looked at her watch and saw that she had been asleep for an hour. She jumped to her feet. Rauwerd must have left by now; he wouldn't have seen her there on his way out. She hurried to the porter's lodge and found another man there.

'Dr van Kempler,' she began, 'has he gone? I'm his wife—I've been waiting for him, but I fell asleep.' This didn't sound quite right. She began again, 'He wasn't expecting me, and I've been sitting on that seat by the statues.'

'Really can't say, madam. There's a conference on and there's doctors going to and fro ...

'He's tall and rather large with fair hair.'

He sucked his teeth and thought. 'Well, I do remember a very big man—I thought to myself at the time, "There's a big man", but that could have been yesterday ...'

She would have to go home; he might already be there. On the other hand he could still be in the hospital. She asked, 'The consultants' room—where is it? I'll just make sure that he's not there before I go home.'

'Well, I don't know that I can let you go there, madam. It's private like, you see.'

He was friendly, but she could see that he was going to be firm about it. Desperation made her cunning. 'Oh, well, I'll sit here for a little longer. Thank you for your help.' She smiled at him and went back to the seat and stayed there until she saw him turn his back to attend to the switchboard.

She was down the passage alongside the statues before he turned round again. The passage went on and on, lined with large mahogany doors—Hospital Secretary, Lady Social Worker, General Office ... there was no end to them. At its end there was another passage, much wider and winding into a dimly distant curve. The first door said 'Hospital Governors' and the second, 'Board Room', and the third said 'Consultants' Room'. She fetched up before it, breathless from hurrying and fear of being caught. Without pausing, in case her fear took over, she knocked on the door and went in.

There were five persons in the room. Three were strangers to her; the fourth was the tall, thin man who had been kind to her at the geriatric hospital—

Rauwerd had called him Dick. The fifth was Rauwerd.

They turned to look at her with unhurried calm, although Rauwerd's calm was shattered by such a fierce delight at the sight of her that she found herself trembling.

He came towards her. 'Tilly, what a delightful surprise!' He took her hands in his, smiling down at her. 'Come and meet some of my colleagues.'

They shook hands with her warmly and Dick said, 'I was so delighted to hear of your marriage. I hope that when I come to Holland you will let me visit you?'

Matilda, struggling with all the sensations of someone who had expected one thing and become involved in another, murmured politely, exchanged small talk with the gentlemen, very much aware that Rauwerd's hand on her arm was sending delightful thrills up it. She listened with apparent interest while one of the learned gentlemen, grey haired and bearded, told her about his recent visit to Leiden, all the while wondering what she was going to say to Rauwerd and, for that matter, what he was going to say to her.

It seemed an age, although it was barely ten minutes before Rauwerd said easily, 'Until ten o'clock tomorrow, then? In the board room?'

They all shook hands again and she went ahead of Rauwerd to the door. She couldn't trust herself to look at him but walked silently beside him back along the corridors and passages to the entrance. The hall was empty, save for the porter reading his paper over a cup of tea. Half-way to the door Rauwerd stopped, took her in his arms and kissed her soundly, and then walked on again, his arm tucked into hers. It took only a few moments to reach the car, just time enough for her to ask, 'Why did you do that?'

He paused, his hand on the car door. 'Because I love you, my dearest Tilly; it is something I have wanted to do since the moment we met—I fell in love with you then.'

He opened the car door and shoved her gently in and then got in beside her.

She said in a voice she strove to keep normal, 'But I didn't like you very much . . .'

He glanced at her sideways, his eyes gleaming in his calm face. 'No, I know that. That is why I suggested our marriage should be on a friendly footing—to give you time to change your opinion of me.'

Matilda digested this remark slowly and with mounting excitement. She wanted to sing aloud, fling her arms around Rauwerd's neck. Everything she had been wanting to tell him bubbled up on to her tongue, but she clenched her teeth; it was neither the time nor the place to do any of these things. She kept silent until he stopped before the house and then skipped ahead of him through the door Cribbs was holding open.

'Tea, madam?' asked Cribbs, so that she was forced to stop and answer him.

'Oh, yes please, Cribbs.'

She glanced at Rauwerd who smiled and said blandly, 'In half an hour, my dear? In the study, perhaps. And we don't want to be interrupted, Cribbs. Keep all the phone calls unless it's something urgent, will you?'

He crossed the hall and opened the study door and Matilda went past him into the centre of the room. She turned to face him almost as soon as he closed the door.

'I went to see Nikky,' she began.

'I thought that you might do that.' He sounded unconcerned and she felt a prick of peevishness.

'Why should you think that?'

'You're my wife, and, even though you weren't aware of it, you were in love with me—still are, I hope.' He crossed the room and took her hands in his. 'Although you didn't know that for a long time, did you?'

She stared up at him. 'No, no I didn't and when I did, I thought that you and Nikky loved each other—she told me . . .'

'My dearest love, if I were to tell you, just once, that I have never loved, nor ever shall love Nikky, would you believe me, so that the whole tiresome thing can be forgotten? There are so many other things I would rather talk about and we have wasted so much time.'

He drew her close in a satisfying, gentle hug and kissed her. 'Can't I ever talk about her again?' demanded Matilda into his shoulder.

'Well, perhaps when I am an old man and you are a delightful old lady, we might discuss it, but not, of course, when the grandchildren are around.'

'But we haven't any children,' observed Matilda, unaware of the silliness of the remark.

'Easily remedied, my darling.'

She leaned back to look into his face. 'I think I'm going to cry,' she said in a watery voice. Then, when she saw the look of love and tenderness in his face, she added, 'But I don't think I will.'

She put up her face to be kissed instead; so much

more pleasant. Indeed, she was enjoying it so much that she didn't hear Cribbs come softly in with the tea tray, and, after a swift pleased look, go softly out again.

Can you keep a secret?

You can keep this one plus 4 free novels

MAIL-IN-OFFER
OFFER CERTIFICATE ✂----

I have enclosed the required number of proofs of purchase from any specially marked "Gifts From The Heart" Harlequin romance book, plus cash register receipts and a check or money order payable to Harlequin Gifts From The Heart Offer, to cover postage and handling.

002

CHECK ONE	ITEM	# OF PROOFS OF PURCHASE	POSTAGE & HANDLING FEE
	01 Brass Picture Frame	2	$ 1.00
	02 Heart-Shaped Candle Holders with Candles	3	$ 1.00
	03 Heart-Shaped Keepsake Box	4	$ 1.00
	04 Gold-Plated Heart Pendant	5	$ 1.00
	05 Collectors' Doll Limited quantities available	12	$ 2.75

NAME _____

STREET ADDRESS _____ APT. # _____

CITY _____ STATE _____ ZIP _____

Mail this certificate, designated number of proofs of purchase (inside back page) and check or money order for postage and handling to:

Gifts From The Heart, P.O. Box 4814
Reidsville, N. Carolina 27322-4814

NOTE THIS IMPORTANT OFFER'S TERMS

Requests must be postmarked by May 31, 1988. Only proofs of purchase from specially marked "Gifts From The Heart" Harlequin books will be accepted. This certificate plus cash register receipts and a check or money order to cover postage and handling must accompany your request and may not be reproduced in any manner. Offer void where prohibited, taxed or restricted by law. LIMIT ONE REQUEST PER NAME, FAMILY, GROUP, ORGANIZATION OR ADDRESS. Please allow up to 8 weeks after receipt of order for shipment. Offer only good in the U.S.A. Hurry—Limited quantities of collectors' doll available. Collectors' dolls will be mailed to first 15,000 qualifying submitters. All other submitters will receive 12 free previously unpublished Harlequin books and a postage & handling refund.

OFFER-1RR

Deep in the heart of Africa lay mankind's most
awesome secret. Could they find Eden . . .
and the grave of Eve?

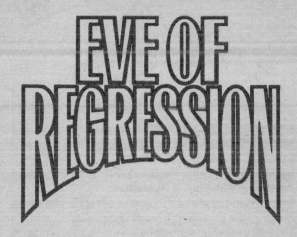

JOHN ARTHUR LONG

A spellbinding novel that combines a fascinating
premise with all the ingredients of an edge-of-the-seat
read: passion, adventure, suspense and danger.

GIFTS FROM THE HEART

from Harlequin

FREE BY MAIL With proofs of purchase
plus postage and handling

A. Hand-polished solid brass picture frame 1-5/8" × 1-3/8" with 2 proofs of purchase.

B. Individually handworked, pair of heart-shaped glass candle holders (2" diameter), 6" candles included, with 3 proofs of purchase.

C. Heart-shaped porcelain keepsake box (1" high) with delicate flower motif with 4 proofs of purchase.

D. Radiant gold-plated heart pendant on 16" chain with complimentary satin pouch with 5 proofs of purchase.

E. Beautiful collectors' doll with genuine porcelain face, hands and feet, and a charming heart appliqué on dress with 12 proofs of purchase. Limited quantities available. See offer terms.

HERE IS HOW TO GET YOUR FREE GIFTS

Send us the required number of proofs of purchase (below) of specially marked "Gifts From The Heart" Harlequin books and cash register receipts with the Offer Certificate (available in the back pages) properly completed, plus a check or money order (do not send cash) payable to Harlequin Gifts From The Heart Offer. We'll RUSH you your specified gift. Hurry—Limited quantities of collectors' doll available. See offer terms.

201R

GIFTS FROM THE HEART
ONE PROOF
OF PURCHASE

To collect your free gift by mail you must include the necessary number of proofs of purchase with order certificate.